*Samuel French Acting Edition*

# Jasper in Deadland

*Book by*
Hunter Foster &
Ryan Scott Oliver

*Music & Lyrics by*
Ryan Scott Oliver

*Additional Orchestrations by*
Solomon Hoffman

---

### FOR PRODUCTION ENQUIRIES

#### UNITED STATES AND CANADA
Info@SamuelFrench.com
1-866-598-8449

#### UNITED KINGDOM AND EUROPE
Plays@SamuelFrench.co.uk
020-7255-4302

Each title is subject to availability from Samuel French, depending upon country of performance. Please be aware that *JASPER IN DEADLAND* may not be licensed by Samuel French in your territory. Professional and amateur producers should contact the nearest Samuel French office or licensing partner to verify availability.

---

*JASPER IN DEADLAND* premiered at Prospect Theatre Company in 2014 in New York City. The Director was Brandon Ivie, with musical direction by Ryan Fielding Garrett, choreography by Lorin Latarro, scenic design by Patrick Rizzotti, costume design by Bobby Pearce, lighting design by Herrick Goldman, and sound design by Ed Chapman. The Stage Manager was Brian R. Sekinger. The cast was as follows:

| | |
|---|---|
| JASPER | Matt Doyle |
| GRETCHEN/AGNES/EURYDICE | Allison Scagliotti |
| MR. LETHE & OTHERS | Ben Crawford |
| PERSEPHONE & OTHERS | Andi Alhadeff |
| PLUTO & OTHERS | Leo Ash Evens |
| AMMUT & OTHERS | Danyel Fulton |
| THE CHUCKSTER/LOKI/OTHERS | F. Michael Haynie |
| LESTER & OTHERS | John-Michael Lyles |
| BEATRIX/HEL/OTHERS | Bonnie Milligan |

*JASPER IN DEADLAND* was subsequently presented at The 5th Avenue Theatre (David Armstrong, Executive Producer and Artistic Director; Bernadine Griffin, Managing Director; Bill Berry, Producing Artistic Director) on May 21, 2015 in Seattle, Washington. The Director was Brandon Ivie, with musical direction by R.J. Tancioco, choreography by Lorin Latarro, set design by Jason Sherwood, costume design by Pete Rush, lighting design by Robert J. Aguilar, and sound design by Justin Stasiw. The Stage Manager was Amy Gornet.

| | |
|---|---|
| JASPER | Matt Doyle |
| GRETCHEN/AGNES | Sydney Shepherd |
| MR. LETHE | Louis Hobson |
| PERSEPHONE & OTHERS | Andi Alhadeff |
| PLUTO & OTHERS | Evan Woltz |
| AMMUT & OTHERS | Brandi Chavonne Massey |
| BEATRIX | Caety Sagoian |
| LITTLE LU & OTHERS | Jared Michael Brown |
| VIRGIL & OTHERS | Kyle Robert Carter |
| HEL & OTHERS | Sarah Rose Davis |
| DANTE & OTHERS | Frederick Hagreen |
| EURYDICE & OTHERS | Diana Huey |
| ENSEMBLE | Kyle Bernbach, Taryn Darr |

*JASPER IN DEADLAND* was originally commissioned by the Pasadena Musical Theatre Company (2011).

# CHARACTERS

JASPER

GRETCHEN / AGNES

EURYDICE

MR. LETHE

PERSEPHONE

PLUTO

AMMUT

LOKI

BEATRIX

HEL

VIRGIL

CERBERUS (THREE HEADS)

DANTE

LITTLE LU

BRUTUS

SISYPHUS

SOME DOUCHE

BLIND JUSTICE

LETHE'S GIRLS

DAUGHTERS OF DANAUS

FACTORY WORKERS / CORPSES / CITIZENS / THE RIVER LETHE

**OTHER CHARACTERS:** The Goddess, Boatman, Anniversary Guy, Mom, Principal Bea, Coach Lewis, Counselor Amanda, Missy, Chaz, Dad, Graham, Agneses, Corpses, Lethe's Girls, Randy, Some Douche, Tourists, Paperboy, Informed Citizens, Irma, Tabloid Girls, Jessica's Mother, Abigail Acrimone, Hathaway, Bartender, Hookah Smokers, Clubbers, Shady, Boss Rhadamanthus, Osiris, Screaming Man, etc.

**Note on Casting:** All roles may be played by any gender. Some roles should have pronouns changed and others should not, regardless of the gender of the actor playing them. Some roles have alternative keys offered (at no additional charge) depending on the voice type of the actor playing them.

Jasper should change pronouns throughout the script to the pronouns of the actor playing the role; the name should not be changed.

Lethe should change pronouns throughout the script to the pronouns of the actor playing the role; the name SHOULD be changed to Madame Lethe or Mx. Lethe.

All other characters should keep the pronouns in the script and should not change the name of the characters (mostly because they are based in mythology). This also includes Agnes/Gretchen.

# SETTING

The living world and the five circles of Deadland.

# MUSICAL NUMBERS

# ACT ONE

## Scene One: Up here

***[MUSIC NO. 01 "GOODBYE, JASPER!"]***

*(Lights rise sharply on a line of characters at the edge of the stage. Note that each line begins simultaneously with the end of the previous line.)*

**MOM.** Three C's two B's and an F Jasper. You wanna be a failure, like your crack-head father? Do you? Tell me?

**PRINCIPAL BEA.** Tell me why you haven't shown up to school in two days. Where have you been and what's this trouble at home I hear about, Jasper?

**COACH LEWIS.** Jasper, why weren't you at swim practice? Strike three, you are off the team!

**COUNSELOR AMANDA.** Off the team! Jasper, your teachers and I were counting on that swimming scholarship! I just don't understand.

**MISSY.** I just don't understand. I mean, I think you're cute, but all you want to do is hang out with Agnes.

**CHAZ.** Agnes? Really? Dude, she is way out of your league. You're such a pill.

**DAD.** Pill. Just one pill, Jasper. Just give me one. Your mother's leaving me… I can't take it. Help me!

**GRAHAM.** Help me understand what it is you have to offer my daughter. You're in a broken home. Bad grades. No hope. No future. Stay away from Agnes, do you understand?

**MOM.** Do you understand why I'm leaving… I've given you my life for seventeen years. Now, I want a life of my own.

**ALL SOLOS**. Jasper.

> *(Lights rise on a bedroom.* **JASPER** *is on the edge
> of the bed with his head in his hands. There is a
> figure under the covers, her face obscured –* **AGNES**.
> *She stirs, and he sings to her.)*

**JASPER**.
> AGNES.
> YOU'RE PERFECT, AGNES.
> I DON'T DESERVE YOU,
> NO WAY.
> MY LIFE'S TOO MESSED UP,
> YOU'LL SEE.
> YOU'LL SEE.

**AGNES**. *(Voice-over)* I love you, Jasper. Do you love me?

> *(Music plays.* **JASPER** *doesn't, can't respond.
> Thump thump, heart beat. Broken,* **AGNES** *rushes
> out, as we hear a voicemail.)*

*(Voicemail voice-over.)* Hey, *It's Agnes…* We need to talk
about last night. I wish you picked up. If you wanna
talk, I will be at our cliff. I'm scared of this cliff, and
you're scared of us. So, I'm jumping in… To show you
I'm not going to be afraid anymore… And when I see
you after… Maybe you won't be afraid of us.

> *(***JASPER** *appears at the cliff.)*

**JASPER**. Agnes. Agnes? I'm at the cliff, just like you said!
Where are you? …Look! You deserve so much more
than me! You just don't understand. My parents'
divorce; I've just seen first hand how it all ends up!
Agnes! *(Becomes suddenly concerned, realizing, looking over
the cliff. He sees something! Did she jump?)* …Agnes? …Oh
God.

> *(There is a slow, audible gasp/inhale from
> somewhere.)*

**VOICES**. *(Inhale.)*
> AHH, AHH, AHH…

**JASPER.** AGNES?! I'm coming!

> *(Music swells.* **JASPER** *dives as – a swinging punk guitar groove, a little sadistic, blares – and suddenly* **JASPER** *is falling…endlessly…into another world.)*

**THE GODDESS.** *(Voice-over.)* Now entering: DEADLAND. Deadland –

**JASPER'S MEMORIES.** Hah!

**JASPER.** AHHHHHHHHH –!

> *(***JASPER*** *falling –)*

**RIVER LETHE.**
BYE! GOODBYE!
GOODBYE! GOODBYE!
GOODBYE! GOODBYE!
GOODBYE! GOODBYE! YUH!
JASPER, GOODBYE!

> *(Time slows and* **JASPER** *seems to float weightless in air. Several young* **WOMEN** *appear to* **JASPER**, *clutching blood-red hoodies. One speaks to him.)*

**JASPER.** What the hell. What's happening?

**SEVERAL AGNESES.**
JASPER! YOU'RE FALLING.

**AGNES #3.** And as you fall into this mythical world, your life will flash before your eyes.

**JASPER.** Where is Agnes?

**SEVERAL AGNESES.** We are Agnes.

**AGNES #5.** Agnes.

**AGNES #7.** Agnes.

**AGNES #3.** Agnes.

**AGNES #4.** Agnes.

**AGNES #2.** Agnes.

**AGNES #6.** Agnes.

**AGNES #4.** Now Jasper, you will see your most *important* memories of you and Agnes.

*(She puts on the red hoodie.)*

**RIVER LETHE.**

YA TA TA DA DA TA TA DA:
THE DAY YOU MET!

> **(JASPER** *encounters a series of memories, each one
> appearing with every flash of light/ding.)*

> **(JASPER** *with a backpack, trailing an* **AGNES***:)*

**JASPER.** Excuse me! Hey! Um…

"AGNES"?
WHAT'S YOUR REAL FIRST NAME?
OH, IT'S AGNES.
HOLY SHIT.
SORRY, I'M NEW IN TOWN…

AND, AGNES,
THIS MAY COME OFF LAME,
BUT AGNES…
GOT NO FRIENDS.
IF YOU'D HANG, I'D BE DOWN?
SAY SOMETHING, AGNES.
SO QUIET, AGNES,
DON'T SMILE, AGNES!

**AGNES #2.**

GOODBYE, JASPER GOODBYE.
YOU'RE A WEIRD GUY,
BUT I THINK I'LL KEEP YOU AROUND.
I'M FREE TOMORROW PAST THREE.
LET'S DO SOMETHING

**ALL AGNESES.**

WONDERFUL.

> *(Time resumes and* **JASPER** *is falling again!)*

**RIVER LETHE.**

BYE! GOODBYE!
GOODBYE! GOODBYE!
GOODBYE! GOODBYE!
GOODBYE! GOODBYE! YUH!
JASPER, GOODBYE!

*(Time slows, **JASPER** floats again in a new memory and a new red-hoodied **AGNES #3**.)*

**RIVER LETHE.**

YA TA TA DA DA TA TA DA:
THE DAY AT THE CLIFF!

*(Ding.)*

**JASPER.**

AGNES,
TAKE THE JUMP WITH ME!
C'MON AGNES,
IT'S NOT HIGH!
IT'S LIKE THIRTY AT MOST?
WE'LL GO STROKE BY STROKE BY STROKE BY STROKE,
AGNES!
COME WITH ME, AGNES!
JUST ONE TIME, AGNES!

**AGNES #3.**

GOODBYE JASPER, GOODBYE.
NICE TRY,
BUT I THINK I'LL STAY ON THE GROUND.
TAKE THE DIVE. I HOPE YOU SURVIVE.
GO ON, MISTER WONDERFUL.

**RIVER LETHE.**

BYE, GOODBYE, GOODBYE, BYE, GOODBYE
OOH…

*(**JASPER** dives into water, and everything becomes soft and blue.)*

**JASPER.**

WEIGHTLESS –
I'M WEIGHTLESS DOWN HERE.

**AGNES #4.** *(Above him, he can't hear…)*

THERE ARE THINGS ABOUT ME I WISH I COULD TELL YOU…

**JASPER.**

NO PRESSURE,
NO WAY.
I SAY, NO DISTRACTIONS.
BUT YOU…

**AGNES #4.**

  YOU THINK I'M PERFECT, BUT I'M NOT...

**JASPER.**

  AND WE'RE ALONE

  WE'RE ALONE,

  ALONE,

  ALONE!

  BEST FRIENDS, AND TRUE

  AGNES, ME... AND YOU.

**RIVER LETHE.** *(Quietly, with sympathy.)*

  YA TA TA DA DA TA TA DA:

  THE LAST NIGHT.

    *(Ding.)*

**AGNES #5.** Let's change things. From this moment on, we will do it right, you and me. We will be the first to make it happen. It has to start somewhere, why not tonight? When they look back and they talk about the great couples of all time, we will be up there: Romeo and Juliet, Anthony and Cleopatra, Orpheus and Eurydice...

  AND WE WON'T

  DARE LOOK BACK

**JASPER & ALL THE AGNESES.**

  AND WE WON'T

  DARE LOOK BACK.

    *(He looks into her eyes, seeing her as if for the first time. He grabs the zipper of the red hoodie, but it becomes a nightmare –)*

**AGNES #5.** But you couldn't love her.

**RIVER LETHE.**

  YA TA TA DA DA TA TA DA!

**AGNES #3.**

  AND NOW SHE'S GONE.

**RIVER LETHE.**

  YA TA TA DA DA TA TA DA!

**AGNES #2.**

WHAT'S DONE CAN'T BE UNDONE!

| **RIVER LETHE.** | **JASPER.** |
|---|---|
| YA TA TA DA DA TA TA DA! | No…no… |
| YA TA TA DA DA TA TA DA! | There has to be another way! |
| YA TA TA DA DA TA TA DA! | I can't lose her! |
| | *Stop!* |

**JASPER.**

I'M GONNA FIND HER!

**RIVER LETHE.**

| GOOD LUCK! | **JASPER.** |
|---|---|
| GOODBYE, JASPER GOODBYE! | BYE! GOODBYE! |
| EYES DRY! PUSH THROUGH | GOODBYE! |
| WITH ALL OF YOUR HEART. | STROKE BY STROKE |
| STAY ON TRACK | BY STROKE |
| AND GET THE GIRL BACK – | BY STROKE BY STROKE… |

**RIVER LETHE.**

| NOW IT'S, TIME THAT YOU FIGHT… | |
|---|---|
| TIME FOR LIFE AFTER LIFE | |
| LIFE AFTER LIFE AFTER LIFE | |
| AFTER LIFE AFTER LIFE | **JASPER.** |
| TO | AGNES, JUST WAIT |
| BYE! GOODBYE! | |
| GOODBYE! | AGNES, I'M COMING FAST |
| GOODBYE! GOODBYE! | AND TO ALL OF MY PAST |
| YUH! JASPER, GOODBYE! | GOODBYE! |
| BYE! | |

*(Blackout.)*

## Scene Two: A Ferryboat

### [MUSIC NO. 02 "THE FERRYBOAT"]

(**JASPER** *is slumped, unconscious, in a long ferryboat. The skeletal figure gravely rowing –* **THE BOATMAN** *– wears a red, tassel-cinched robe. Also in the boat is a middle-aged guy in a suit,* **VIRGIL**. *It's the same actor that played Lewis in the first scene.*)

**VIRGIL**. *(Distant at first, but growing more present.)* Hey kid! Wake up, why don'tcha?

*(Looks to* **THE BOATMAN**.)

**JASPER**. Agnes! Where's Agnes?! Wow. That was some nightmare.

**VIRGIL**. Here, have some water.

**RIVER LETHE**.

WATER… WATER… WATER…

**JASPER**. Where am I?

**VIRGIL**.

THE FERRY…

TO DEADLAND.

I'M VIRGIL, THAT'S THE BOATMAN.

**JASPER**. Ahhh!

**VIRGIL**. Ha. Kid, you think that "old softy" is scary…just wait till you see the three-headed dog. Now, let's get you checked in,

CASE NUMBER –

SIGMA J THETA Q TWENTY-SEVEN FOURTEEN.

**JASPER**. This whole thing is probably just some trick, right? Agnes is always doing stuff like this. She makes me think she jumped in and I tried to save her and now she's home laughing her ass off… [You're one of those Duck Boat tours?]* Right? She paid you to come pick me up.

---

*The licensee can substitute any culturally relevant reference here pertaining to the location of their production.

Though it's a little cold down here – considering it's almost springtime…

**RIVER LETHE.**

SPRINGTIME… SPRINGTIME… SPRINGTIME…

**JASPER.** Wait. Is the river…talking…?

**RIVER LETHE.**

TALKING… TALKING… TALKING…

**JASPER.** *Who is doing that?!* Stop repeating me!

**RIVER LETHE.**

PEATING ME… PEATING ME… PEATING ME…

**VIRGIL.** Kid,

THAT'S JUST THE RIVER,

*(spoken)* Mm hmm

SO YOU BEST CATCH YOUR BREATH.

IT'S JUST THE RIVER,

*(spoken)* That's right

NAMED FOR MY BOSS, MR. LETHE…

IT TALKS…

GOT A MIND OF ITS OWN!

*(The boat finally reaches the dock.)*

Well here we are.

**JASPER.** Okay. Weird. I just need to get back home. Is there a bus stop around here?

**VIRGIL.** Oh sure, a bus stop, sure.

*(There is a monstrous howl in the distance…)*

**JASPER.** What's that?!

**VIRGIL.** That? Is *CERBERUS.*

**(VIRGIL** *laughs and the scene moves on.)*

### Scene Three: The Gates of Deadland

*(A beach of red sand, where lay the Gates of Deadland. A starless sky hangs above, swept by a gray channel of clouds. **CERBERUS**, a gigantic three-headed dog, stands ever-alert and ready to attack.)*

**[MUSIC NO. 03 "WHAT IS LIFE"]**

*(The queue of **CORPSES** is revealed, filling out papers on clipboards.)*

**CORPSES.** AHH! AHH!

> *(**CERBERUS** roars. It sounds like a Tyrannosaurus mixed with Godzilla.)*

**CERBERUS HEAD CENTER.** Brothers! Lately I have been feeling – SO EXISTENTIAL.

**CERBERUS HEAD LEFT.** Why, sister?! Obviously, existence is merely guarding the Gates of Deadland for our master, King Pluto! I mean, right?!

**CERBERUS HEAD RIGHT.** No, brother... I think I know what sister means. It isn't OUR existence she wonders about... BUT *HUMAN* EXISTENCE.

**CERBERUS HEAD CENTER.** Perhaps we must think it over together. After all, *three* heads are much better than one...

**CERBERUS (ALL HEADS).**
WHAT IS LIFE? A DISTRACTION? A BATTLE?

**CERBERUS HEAD CENTER.**
WE WONDER IT.

**CERBERUS HEAD LEFT & RIGHT.**
WE WONDER IT.

**CERBERUS (ALL HEADS).**
WHAT IS LIFE?
JUST A CATCH-ALL FOR CATTLE CALLED HUMANS?

**CERBERUS HEAD RIGHT.**
    THEY KNOW IT GOES SO QUICKLY,
**CERBERUS HEAD LEFT.**
    YET, DRAMATIZE IT THICKLY –
**CERBERUS HEAD CENTER.**
    IT MAKES US FEEL SO SICKLY
    JUST HOW FICKLY THEY BEHAVE.
**CERBERUS (ALL HEADS).**
    AS CORPSES COME CAREENING,
    WE'RE HUNGRY FOR LIFE'S MEANING!

    *(Ad-lib laughing.)*

    *(**VIRGIL** addresses the **CORPSES**.)*

**VIRGIL.** Welcome to Deadland… Please step up, state your name and get your Deadland ID And keep it moving!

    *(A long line of people fill out paperwork and then step up, give their cause of death and then feed their paperwork to the dog. They smile awkwardly as their pictures are taken; They are given their IDs and then they exit.)*

**CERBERUS (ALL HEADS).** Cause of Death?

**WOMAN #1.** Drug overdose…

**WOMAN #2.** Car crash.

    *(**ANNIVERSARY GUY** steps up. He has a knife through his head.)*

**ANNIVERSARY GUY.** Forgot our anniversary.

**JASPER.** Um…hi, my name is Jasper –

**CERBERUS (ALL HEADS).** Cause of death?

**JASPER.** *(Trying to be charming.)* Um…you ever have one of those days that starts off one way and then there's a crazy left turn and, you're like, "Wow! How did that happen?"

**CERBERUS (ALL HEADS).** CAUSE OF DEATH?!

**JASPER.** Hey, look, I'm not dead. I am very much alive.

> (*Suddenly* **CERBERUS** *is onto a scent. It sniffs*
> **JASPER** *up and down, then howls in a mania.*)

**CERBERUS & CORPSES.**
ALIVE!
HE'S ALIVE!

**JASPER.** See! Told ya! Now, if you just point me to the nearest bus stop and I'll –

> (*Spots a hoodie on one of the dead.*)

Where'd you get that hoodie?

> (*Grabbing the hoodie.*)

**CORPSE.** Get off! Some hot-ass girl gave it to me.

**JASPER.** That belongs to Agnes. Was she here? Where'd she go?

**CORPSE.** (*Points toward the gates to Deadland.*) In there, dude, through the gates!

**JASPER.** What the hell? Hey…um excuse me! …Look, I need to get through these gates, my friend might be in there –

**CERBERUS HEAD LEFT.** Get through?

**CERBERUS HEAD RIGHT.** A live soul?

**CERBERUS HEAD CENTER.** Through these gates? Ha! I have a better idea…

**CERBERUS (ALL HEADS).**
WHAT IS LIFE?
IF WE EAT YOU,
MIGHT WE KNOW?

> (**CERBERUS** *chases him.*)

**JASPER.** EAT ME? Wait! You can't eat me?

**CERBERUS HEAD CENTER.** *AND WHY NOT?*

**JASPER.** Okay, this isn't happening…

**CERBERUS.** ANSWER US!

**JASPER.** You can't eat me… Because… Because… I know the answer to the question you ask!

**CERBERUS (ALL HEADS).** (*All heads tilt.*) …*YOU DO?*

**JASPER.** What is life? Right? That's what you want to know. Let me through so I can find my friend and I'll tell you everything…

*(He's suddenly filled with frustration, and his fear melts away.)*

**[MUSIC NO. 04 "THE KILLING"]**

**JASPER.**

WHO AM I TO KNOW THE TRUTH?
I'M A LOSER.
WHAT IS LIFE? AND WHY EXIST?
IT WOULD SUCK TO GET DEVOURED,
SO I'LL TRY NOW,
I WILL PITCH THE PAINFUL GIST.

What is life? Life is awful people.

*(The beat kicks in and **JASPER** begins addressing the **CORPSES**.)*

TAKE MY MOTHER FOR A SPIN –
GREAT EXAMPLE!
SIXTEEN YEARS, SHE COOKS AND CLEANS.
TILL SHE WAKES ONE DAY TO THINK,
"WHERE'D THE TIME GO?
IS THIS ALL THAT LIVING MEANS?"

OH, SHE WANTS MORE AND MORE.
THAT'S ALL THAT HUMANS SEEK. YEAH…

| | |
|---|---|
| SHE'S A HUMAN AFTER A<br>    KILLING, | **CORPSES.**<br>HEY! |
| WILLING SHE'LL SNATCH<br>    UP A MOVIE STAR. | |
| SCREW THE WORLD! SHE<br>    NEEDS HIGHER<br>    BILLING – | **CORPSES.**<br>HEY! |
| SPILLING HERSELF FOR<br>    THE CASH AND CAR.<br>SHE'LL DIE POINTING UP<br>    AT HER SHELVES, | |

**JASPER.**
SEE THE PEOPLE, ALL THE
    CRAZY PEOPLE
LIVING, K-K-KILLING
    THEMSELVES.

**CORPSES.**
K-K-KILLING

**CERBERUS (ALL HEADS).**
OOH

**JASPER.**
AND MY FATHER'S JUST AS
    SICK!

**CORPSE SOLO.**
PASS THE PERCOCET!

**JASPER.**
FINDING NEW WAYS TO
    GET DUMB.

**CORPSE SOLO.**
FINDING NEW WAYS TO GET
    MORE

**JASPER.**
THERE ARE SOME WHO
    SEARCH FOR MORE,
BUT MY FATHER DEAR,

**CORPSES.**
MORE MORE

**WOMEN.**
MY FATHER DEAR        MY FATHER DEAR
HE WANTS ONLY TO BE
    NUMB.               WOAH! NO!
OH TELL THIS WORLD       GOODBYE!
    GOODBYE!
GOODBYE!              GOODBYE!
STILL, WHAT'S IT TO ME?

**CORPSES.**
WHAT'S IT TO ME?!

**JASPER.**
HE'S A HUMAN AFTER A
    KILLING,

**CORPSES.**
HEY!

**JASPER.**

    FILLING HIS DAYS WITH
        HOPE TO SCORE.

**CORPSES.**

    OH-OOH YEAH!

**JASPER.**

    CHOKIN' BACK, TILL LIFE
        GETS MORE THRILLING,

**CORPSES.**

    HEY!

| **JASPER.** | **CORPSES.** |
|---|---|
| CHILLING HIS DRINKS,<br>  KNOWIN' NOT WHO<br>  FOR. | KNOWIN' NOT WHO FOR |
| | **CORPSES.** |
| HE'LL DIE, STARING OFF AT<br>  LOST GOALS… | OOH… OFF AT LOST |

**CORPSES.**

    AHH-AH!

**JASPER.**

    SEE THE PEOPLE, ALL THE
        CRAZY PEOPLE,

| | **CORPSES.** |
|---|---|
| **JASPER.** | AH! |
| LIVING, K-K-KILLING THEIR<br>  SOULS. | K-K-KILLING |

**CERBERUS HEAD #1.** If you think life is that terrible then maybe you ended up in the right place.

**JASPER.**

    MOST PEOPLE ARE EITHER "A" OR "B."
    EXCEPT AGNES, 'CAUSE SEE…
    AGNES SHOWED ME MORE THAN A KILLING,

**JASPER.**

| DRILLING HER WORDS MY<br>  LIFE'S NOT A WASTE. | **WOMEN.** |
|---|---|
| AGNES SAYS, IT CAN BE<br>  FULFILLING | IT CAN BE FULFILLING |

**JASPER.**

> SHE'S SHILLING A TRUTH
>     THAT I HAVEN'T FACED:
> THAT I'LL DIE, WASTING
>     ALL OF MY TIME…
> *(Then, aggressive again!)*

**JASPER.**

> SEE THE CORPSES AFTER A
>     KILLING,

**MEN.**

> SEE THE CORPSES! HEY!

**JASPER.**

> TRILLING THE COIL WE
>     LIVE MORTALLY.
>
> THIS IS LIFE! MINDLESSLY
>     MILLING

**CORPSES.**

> TRILLING THE COIL WE LIVE
>     MORTALLY.
> OH-OOH YEAH!
> THIS IS LIFE!

**CORPSES.**

> HEY!

**JASPER.**

> FULFILLING MY FEAR, THAT
>     THE WORST IS ME.
> I WON'T DIE AND BE THAT
>     GUY
> WHO LIKE THEM WASTED
>     THIS CLIMB…!

**CORPSES.**

> WE WASTED THIS CLIMB!

**JASPER.**

> I'LL SAVE YOU AGNES, I
>     WILL SAVE YOU AGNES

**CORPSES.**

> GET THE GIRL BACK
> JASPER, GET THE GIRL BACK

**JASPER.**

> YEAH! LIVING, WELL
>     TRYING,
> I'LL GET HER BACK AND
>     PROVE
> I'M NOT JUST K-K-KILLING

**CORPSES.**

> LIVING, DYING
>
> GET HER BACK
>
> PROVE WE'RE NOT JUST!

**JASPER.**
 MY TIME!

**JASPER.**
 OUR TIME!

**CORPSES.**
 GET THE GIRL BACK
 JASPER, GET THE GIRL BACK!
 GET THE GIRL BACK
 JASPER, GET THE GIRL BACK!

**CORPSES.**
 GET THE GIRL BACK
 JASPER, GET THE GIRL BACK!

  *(The heads of* **CERBERUS** *consider this. Then…)*

  *[MUSIC NO. 05 "MARK THIS!"]*

**CERBERUS.** Thank you for the truth.
 FOR ENLIGHTENING US, YOU MAY ENTER THE GATE, BUT
  MARK THIS.

**JASPER.** Marking!

**CERBERUS.**
 DEADLAND IS A PLACE WHERE YOU FORGET LIFE!
 ALREADY, YOU'VE BEGUN TO FORGET YOUR OWN!
 IF YOU REMAIN TOO LONG, YOU'LL FORGET LIFE
  COMPLETELY,
 AND JOIN THE DEAD FOREVER.

 YOU MAY ENTER!

  *(The world goes silent waiting for* **JASPER***'s next move.)*

**JASPER.** Do I just – uh?

**CERBERUS.** ENTER!

**VIRGIL.** Good luck with your girlfriend!

**JASPER.** She's not my girlfriend!

  *(***JASPER** *enters the gates.)*

## Scene Four: The City Circle Streets

*(Lights shift as we enter Deadland. The City Circle Streets: the main street of a most spectacular city. At ends classic and nouveau, its steel spires and silver skyscrapers stand proudly on pale marble streets; a perfect high-noon sun beams down.* **JASPER** *looks in awe at the city.)*

*[MUSIC NO. 06 "THE CITY CIRCLE"]*

*(Suddenly the sky becomes a Jumbotron, and a commercial airs.)*

**MR. LETHE.** *("On screen.")*
WELCOME –!
TO DEADLAND –!
YOU'RE HERE, IN CITY CIRCLE!

> *(Wicked drum solo.)*

**MR. LETHE.** *("On screen.")*
WELCOME –!

**LETHE'S GIRLS.** *("On screen.")*
WELCOME –!

**MR. LETHE.** *("On screen.")*
TO DEADLAND –!

**LETHE'S GIRLS.** *("On screen.")*
DEADLAND –!

**MR. LETHE.** *("On screen.")*
GET TO KNOW ME, MR. LETHE!

Citizens of the City Circle, this is your friendly Mr. Lethe, reminding you to *stay hydrated!* Water from the River Lethe is scientifically proven to keep you feelin' nice and bright all day long! And considering time is all relative – a day's a year, a decade's a second – consider that promise as good as eternity. 'Cause don't forget...

**LETHE'S GIRLS.** *("On screen.")*
LETHE IS MORE...!

> *(The commercial disappears, **JASPER** is wandering around looking at the city. Suddenly a cluster of* **TOURISTS** *holding maps and taking pictures peel on with* **GRETCHEN** *– a tour guide.)*

### [MUSIC NO. 06A "TOUR SONG"]

**GRETCHEN.**
> NOW IS THE AWESOME PART OF THE TOUR,
> COOL SHIT THAT NEVER MADE THE LAME BROCHURE
> BROUGHT TO YOU FREE
> BY YOUR AWESOME GUIDE, ME, BUT TIPS ARE APPRECIATED
> – AND I'M TALKING COLD HARD CASH FOLKS, NOT ME
> LIFTING UP MY SHIRT FOR FIVE SECONDS RANDY.

**RANDY.** Sorry.

**GRETCHEN.**
> NOW ON YOUR RIGHT IS THE FAMED CLOCK TOWER.

**TOURISTS.** Ooooh.

> *(They snap photos.)*

**GRETCHEN.**
> NOTE THAT THE HANDS DON'T TELL THE HOUR,

**TOURISTS.** Ahhh.

> *(They snap photos.)*

**GRETCHEN.**
> BECAAAAAUSE
> WHILE WE'RE CONVENING HERE,
> TIME HAS NO MEANING HERE,
> AND YOU'RE DEAD FOREVER AND YOU'LL NEVER SEE YOUR
> KIDS AGAIN,
> WHICH IS OKAY 'CAUSE KIDS SUCK!

**JASPER.** Excuse me –

**GRETCHEN.** Yes, Eddie Munster.

**JASPER.** Um… Miss, uh…

> *(Looking at the tag on her shirt.)*

**GRETCHEN.** Gretchen –

JASPER. Gretchen! Hi. You see, I'm still alive and I'm looking for a friend of mine and she may be alive, too. I think we're here by mistake.

GRETCHEN. Dude, I'm working.

JASPER. No, no, you don't understand –

>   (JASPER *touches her arm, there is a ding, and a special nearby illuminates a memory, which only the* GRETCHEN *can see.)*

SOME DOUCHE. *(Sung like a stupid recitative.)*
HEY! I GOT YOUR TEXT THIS MORNING, YOU SENT IT AT LIKE 4 A.M. –

GRETCHEN. Ahhh! Who is that douche? Why is he here?

SOME DOUCHE.
YOU WERE WASTED WEREN'T YOU? YOU WERE! I KNEW IT!

JASPER. Wait, who's here?

GRETCHEN. Nobody…it must just be a memory…

SOME DOUCHE.
DO YOU WANNA SEE A PIC OF MY JUNK?

>   (GRETCHEN *is zapped back to reality.)*

GRETCHEN. Woah dude! I think when you touched me you put stuff in my head! I think that was a memory from my life. I just saw like, my boyfriend or something…

JASPER. Can you help me?

GRETCHEN. *(Giving him a map.)* Here take a map. Now, Goodbye!

JASPER. Wait!

TOURIST. I think that's him!

TOURIST. The alive boy!

TOURIST. Let's take a picture!

>   *(They start taking pictures of* JASPER.*)*

>   **[MUSIC NO. 07 "JASPER IN DEADLAND"]**

>   *(The group exits as a* PAPERBOY *runs onstage.)*

**PAPERBOY**. Extra extra! Living boy turns city upside down!
His mere touch makes us remember
THE LIVES WE'VE FORGOTTEN.

**PAPERBOY**.
JASPER IN DEADLAND!

**INFORMED CITIZEN #1**. *(Reading.)*
"A LIVING SOUL AMONG US,

**PAPERBOY**.
JASPER IN DEADLAND!

**INFORMED CITIZEN #1**. *(Reading.)*
LIVE TEEN EMBARKS ON QUEST."

**INFORMED CITIZEN #2**.
"FOR A BEST FRIEND,
HE CALLS AGNES…"
SHE'S LOST, HE'S HERE:

**INFORMED CITIZENS #1 & #2**.
I'M OBSESSED!
WITH JASPER IN DEADLAND!

**PAPERBOY**.
BUY A COPY, READ THE REST.

**JASPER**. *(Stopping* **INFORMED CITIZEN #1**.*)* 'Scuse me, sir. Can you help me?

> **(INFORMED CITIZEN #1** *tries walking past but bumps* **JASPER** *– Ding. A gorgeous woman in blue light appears, seen only to* **INFORMED CITIZEN #1**.*)*

**INFORMED CITIZEN #1**. Irma the Clubgirl…

**IRMA**.
HAPPY TWENTY-FIRST BIRTHDAY, HAROLD.

**INFORMED CITIZEN #1**. I'd forgotten all about her!

**IRMA**.
IT'S TWO DOLLARS FOR A LAP DANCE, AND THEN FIVE
DOLLARS FOR A TOE SUCK,

**INFORMED CITIZEN #1**. *(Covering the memory up as it fades away.)* Aw, kid – I dunno how you did that…but thanks for giving this old sop something he'd like to remember! Gee! *(Goes off.)*

> *(Lights shift. Two girls reading tabloids enter. They are drinking water. One alerts the other upon catching* **JASPER**.*)*

**TABLOID GIRL #1.**

THAT'S JASPER.

**TABLOID GIRL #2.** *(Buried.)*

HM?

**TABLOID GIRL #1.**

IN DEADLAND.

**TABLOID GIRL #2.**

WHAT?

**TABLOID GIRL #1.**

THE FLIPPIN' COVER STORY

**TABLOID GIRL #2.** *(Gasp, exclaims.)*

IT'S JASPER!

**TABLOID GIRL #1.**

SHHH!

**TABLOID GIRL #2.** *(Quiet.)*

IN DEADLAND…

**TABLOID GIRL #1.**

HE'S CUTER THAN HIS PIC.

**TABLOID GIRL #2.**

IF HE CAN'T FIND THIS GIRL, "AGNES,"

**TABLOID GIRLS #1 & #2.**

I BET I COULD DO THE TRICK!

**TABLOID GIRL #1.**

HEY, JASPER-IN-DEADLAND!
CAN I TOUCH YOUR HAIR?

**JASPER.** Look, I need to find Agnes –

> *(She touches his hair. Ding. Another memory.)*

**JESSICA'S MOTHER.**
VALEDICTORIAN! WHAT A MITZVAH, JESSICA! IT'S JUST A PITY THAT POOR CHARLES FELL DOWN THOSE STAIRS, BUT... I ALWAYS BELIEVED YOU WERE MEANT TO BE THE TOP OF YOUR CLASS! MAZEL TOV.

**TABLOID GIRL #1 (JESSICA).** *(All according to plan.)* Die, Charles. Die.

**TABLOID GIRL #2.** So, what does she look like, this Agnes?

**JASPER.** Well, she's got brown hair... Or is it red? Or black? Wait. Why can't I remember? I am having a hard time remembering what she looks like!

> *(Vulturous TV reporter* **ABIGAIL ACRIMONE** *bursts onto the street with her bumbling* **CAMERAGUY.***)*

**TABLOID GIRL #2.** Then how do you know she's not me?

**TABLOID GIRL #1.** Or me.

**PAPERBOY.** Or me.

**JASPER.** I'll take my chances.

**ABIGAIL ACRIMONE.** This is Abigail Acrimone *[uh-KRIMM-uh-NEE]* for Deadline News. We're here with the boy everyone's talking about, Living Boy Jasper. Welcome. *(Gives mic, pulls back.)* Jasper, your touch makes Dead Citizens recall memories of forgotten lives, destroying the delicate line between life and death. How does it feel to be a monster?

**JASPER.** What?

**ABIGAIL ACRIMONE.** *(Gives mic, pulls back.)* And if Agnes is out there watching, do you have anything you'd like to say to her? *(Gives mic, pulls back, but* **JASPER** *grabs it.)*

**JASPER.** Agnes! I'm here! I found your red hoodie, see? If you're out there watching, come find me at –

**ABIGAIL ACRIMONE.** All right Chatty Cathy, let's get to some viewer questions! Montana asks.

> *(***JASPER** *sees a young* **GIRL** *who could look like* **AGNES.** *She drops a red knit cap.* **JASPER** *runs and grabs it, but the* **GIRL** *is gone in a sea of* **REPORTERS** *and* **JASPER GROUPIES.***)*

**ABIGAIL ACRIMONE.**
JASPER, TELL DEADLAND
DO YOU MEAN TO RESURRECT US?

**INFORMED CITIZEN #1.** *(Coming onto the scene.)*
JASPER!

**ABIGAIL ACRIMONE.**
JASPER,

**INFORMED CITIZEN #1.**
HERE, JASPER.

**ABIGAIL ACRIMONE.**
NO HERE, KID.

| **INFORMED CITIZEN #1.** | **ABIGAIL ACRIMONE.** |
|---|---|
| HOW IS IT | |
| YOU AFFECT US? | KID, I'M HERE, HELLO? |

**TABLOID GIRL #2.**
JASPER!

| **ABIGAIL.** | **PAPERBOY.** | **INFORMED CITIZEN #1.** |
|---|---|---|
| JASPER! | JASPER | JASPER! |
| | IN | |
| | DEADLAND | |

**ABIGAIL & INFORMED CITIZEN #1.**
HEY.

**TABLOID GIRL #2.**
IT'S ME YOUR BEST PAL, AGNES!

| **ABIGAIL.** | **INF. CIT. #1.** | **TAB. GIRL #1.** | **PAPERBOY.** |
|---|---|---|---|
| TELL THE | TELL THE | WHAT? | EXTRA! |
| CITY, KID: | CITY, KID: | | JASPER IN |
| | | NO SHE'S | DEADLAND |
| | | NOT. | |

| **ABIGAIL.** | **INF. CIT. #1.** | **TAB. GIRL #1.** | **TAB. GIRL #2.** |
|---|---|---|---|
| ARE YOU | | | |
| HOPELESS? | ARE YOU | I'M AGNES, | I'M AGNES, |
| | SCARED? | YOU'RE MY | YOU'RE MY |
| | | BRO! | BRO! |

**ALL BUT JASPER.**
>EV'RY MOMENT
>JASPER'S NEAR US,
>THE LIFE WE FORGOT
>COMES AGLOW…

**TABLOID GIRL #2.** Touch me Jasper, touch me!

**JASPER.** Her hat!

>*(Everybody but* **ABIGAIL ACRIMONE** *dives for* **JASPER**, *who escapes.)*

**ABIGAIL ACRIMONE.**
>WELL, GOOD LUCK
>JASPER-IN-DEADLAND.
>THANKS SO MUCH –
>WHERE'D HE GO?

>*(They all give chase and ad-lib as the scene transitions.)*

## Scene Five: Lethe's Office

*(Lights up on* **MR. LETHE**'s *office. We see him in silhouette or just the back of his chair, but we can't see his face. His assistant,* **HATHAWAY**, *stands before him.)*

**MR. LETHE**. Jasper in Deadland.

**HATHAWAY**. Good afternoon, Mr. Lethe.

**MR. LETHE**. That damn dog! Doesn't realize what he's done. Now, we've got a live soul roaming around Deadland. News of this boy has gone viral! People are in a frenzy!

*(Then, he turns around.)*

Soon as Pluto hooked up the internet down here I knew we were in trouble. If I were running things, I'd unplug us all. Aw… I want to be in charge!

**HATHAWAY**. Oh, sweetheart…

**MR. LETHE**. I helped betray the Titans and look what happens? Jupiter gets the earth, Neptune gets the sea, Pluto gets the underworld and oh… What does Cousin Lethe get for his troubles? A little teensy weensy fucking river!

**HATHAWAY**. A river that's made you rich!

**MR. LETHE**. Yes… But not powerful enough… Hell, I'm wittier than Jupiter.

**HATHAWAY**. Yes, you are!

**MR. LETHE**. *(Stroking his hair.)* I'm sexier than Neptune…

**HATHWAY**. He's just a Mama's boy in skinny jeans!

**MR. LETHE**. I've got better hair than Pluto –

**HATHWAY**. He's got a nasty-ass piece.

**MR. LETHE**. Exactly! Oh, why do I have to work for that idiot?!

*(Then.)*

Oh, Hathaway… One day, I will rule all the Cosmos… And we will circle the sun as I lounge on my "chaise

transat" with you beside me…providing me my trashy
novels, my pink frothy libations, and my SPF 5000…

**HATHAWAY.** My heart beats with anticipation…

**MR. LETHE.** So I'm not going to let this "alive boy" destroy
everything I've built!

### *[MUSIC NO. 08 "JASPER IN DEADLAND (LETHE STYLE)"]*

**MR. LETHE.** Take a note:
JASPER IN DEADLAND.
THIS LIVING BOY IS
    TROUBLE.
WHILE JASPER'S IN
    DEADLAND –
HE'LL MAKE THEIR
    MEM'RIES THRIVE…
YET IF HE SOMEHOW FINDS     **HATHAWAY.**
    THIS…                       Agnes.
"AGNES" …
HE WON'T LEAVE TILL
    SHE'S BROUGHT BACK
    ALIVE.

    *(Then.)*

**MR. LETHE.** Call the Norse Gods and track him down.

**HATHAWAY.** I'll get Hel and Loki right on it!

    **(HATHAWAY** *exits, leaving* **MR. LETHE** *alone.)*

**MR. LETHE.**
"IF JASPER STAYS IN DEADLAND."
MY UNDERWORLD WON'T SURVIVE

    *(The scene transitions.)*

**CHORUS.**
DEAD, DEAD, DEAD, DEAD
DEAD, DEAD, DEAD, DEAD
DEAD, DEAD, DEAD, DEAD

## Scene Six: Elsewhere in the City

(*JASPER arrives at a sign that reads: BEATRIX PORTINARI – AUTOMOBILE ENTHUSIAST, PHILANTROPIST, CITY ADMINISTRATOR AND CHAMPION WATER SKIER… GONE FOR VACATION.*)

(*Dejected,* **JASPER** *sits at a bar.*)

**GRETCHEN.** Alive boy!

**JASPER.** Tour Girl… *Gretchen.* Good to see you again.

**GRETCHEN.** Cigarette?

**JASPER.** No thanks.

**GRETCHEN.** Yeah, these things will kill you.

**JASPER.** Agh! Sorry, my head is pounding!

**GRETCHEN.** Drink this. It'll take away the headache.

(*Throws him a water bottle.* **JASPER** *downs the water.*)

**JASPER.** It's so chalky…

**GRETCHEN.** It's from The River Lethe. It's the only kind o' water we deadfolk drink.

**JASPER.** Thank you.

**GRETCHEN.** Wow… I've never met anyone "alive" before. You're so dangerous. It's really doing it for me. I'm like, into it, but I'm like, afraid of it… I like, wanna get near you, but I think I wanna stay over here.

**JASPER.** Look, I just need to find Agnes, and get the hell out of here.

**GRETCHEN.** So, tell me…this girl – the fabled Agnes – you love her or what?

**JASPER.** No, I don't love her. We're just friends.

**GRETCHEN.** So you're gay… You're her gay BFF.

**JASPER.** No… I'm not gay… I'm very straight and we're "best friends"…

GRETCHEN. "Best friends" with a girl and you ain't tappin' it? That's a new one…

JASPER. Look, we may have done that, but it didn't mean anything and –

(Then.)

I am not discussing this with you!

GRETCHEN. Listen grumpy-socks, I am a great listener. Like Lucy in the Peanuts; just put a nickel in the can. Chink-chink.

JASPER. Lucy also pulled out the football at the last minute…

GRETCHEN. C'mon! I wanna hear this! We don't get a lot of this goo-goo stuff down here. In fact, it's mostly non-existent.

JASPER. Look. Agnes and I aren't like that. Because, Agnes has everything. Perfect family. Famous doctor for a father… Beautiful stepmom… Agnes is too good for anyone… Me? I have a cheating mother and a drug addict for a father… How could she possibly love me – Look, the best part of my day? I get up every morning and I go for a dive. There's this cliff…it's called…it's called. I can't seem to remember… And I always invite Agnes to come, and she hates to… She jumped in and… Why am I having a hard time…

GRETCHEN. Remembering?

JASPER. Yeah. Ever since I got here…

AGNES. What happens when you can't remember? Exactly?

JASPER. It's weird, it's like there are these pictures of my life on a wall… Except, someone keeps taking them down… Dusty squares and rectangles where my life used to be…

GRETCHEN. It's starting.

**[MUSIC NO. 09 "THE FORGETTING"]**

JASPER. What's starting?

**GRETCHEN**. The forgetting. It happens in phases…

> IT'S A PROCESS.
> FIRST, YOU DIE.
> AS YOU FALL FROM LIFE TO DEATH,
> YOU FALL INTO THE LETHE,
> BOARD THE FERRY,
> PAY YOUR FARE.
> AND YOU THINK, "I HAD A THOUGHT"…
> BUT YOU FORGOT.
> JUST…FORGOT.

The first stage is the headaches.

> SO IT STARTS.
> SMALL DETAILS BEGIN TO BLUR,
> TILL THE PERSON THAT YOU WERE
> SEEMS SO DISTANT.
> WAS THAT YOU?
> AS EACH MEMORY ERASES,
> THE PHOTOS OF FAMILIAR FACES
> SMUDGE AND BLOT –
> BUT YOU WON'T CARE A LOT;
> YOU'LL FORGET YOU FORGOT.

The second stage, you begin to forget others: your friends, your parents. The third stage, you start speaking in Portuguese.

**JASPER**. Portuguese?…

**GRETCHEN**. No one knows why.

> NOW, IT ISN'T UNCOMMON TO
> TRY TO STOP IT, TO FIGHT FOR YOUR LIFE,
> NEVER TO LOSE SIGHT OF YOUR LIFE.
>
> IT'S TRAGICALLY NORMAL TO
> JOT IT DOWN,
> TO WRITE ALL YOUR LIFE,
> GRIPPING TIGHT TO YOUR LIFE.
>
> YOU MAKE NOTES IN A BOOK
> SO TO FIGHT THE FORGETTING,
> YOU MIGHT KEEP THE BEST THINGS,
> AND OMIT WHAT'S UPSETTING,

> BUT AS DAYS PASS YOU LOOK IN YOUR BOOK JUST TO FIND,
> THAT THE BOOK THAT YOU TOOK SERVES ONE PURPOSE:
> TO REMIND YOU OF
> ALL OF THE PEOPLE
> YOU'LL NEVER SEE AGAIN,
> FOR EVEN WHEN THEY COME,
> THEY'LL END UP JUST AS DUMB AND THEN…

The last stage: you forget yourself. And suddenly you feel – okay.

> AT LAST, IT STOPS
> AND YOU TOSS THE BOOK FOR TRASH,
> OR YOU TORCH THE BOOK TO ASH
> JUST LIKE THEY DID
> JUST LIKE ME…
> AND YOU'LL LEARN LIKE OTHER FOLK
> THAT LIFE IS JUST A JOKE,
> A TRICK OF GLASS AND SMOKE;
> A DREAM
> FROM WHICH YOU'VE WOKE…

**JASPER.** So, I have to find her before she forgets who she is OR worse, I forget. This is just great! All I've got to show for this is this dumb red hoodie and this stupid faux vintage knit hat…

**GRETCHEN.** YO – where did you get that?

**JASPER.** I thought I saw her on the street…and then I found this on the pavement when that reporter was after me –

**GRETCHEN.** I have – *TOTALLY* seen that faux vintage knit hat before. I'm like maybe four thousand percent sure.

**JASPER.** You have?! Where?

**GRETCHEN.** I'm sure I've *seen it*, not sure *where*. Maybe at one of the hang outs…?

**JASPER.** Then let's go…

**GRETCHEN.** I can't remember which one…

**JASPER.** Then take me to all of them!

### *[MUSIC NO. 10 "LIVING DEAD"]*

**GRETCHEN.** All right Bucko! I'll take you to all the hot spots! But don't be surprised when we find your friend, if she's having too good a time to leave, 'cause I'm telling you, this city is unplugged like life support!

**JASPER.** That's not funny!

> *(On the street.)*

**GRETCHEN.** It is when you're dead!

> EXCUSE THIS GROTESQUE ACT OF REVELING –
> IT'S JUST IT KILLS ME WHY YOU COME.

**CITIZENS.**
> OOH, IT KILLS ME!
> OOH, IT JUST KILLS ME.

**GRETCHEN & CITIZENS.**
> KILLS ME WHY YOU COME.

**GRETCHEN.**
> THERE'S NO LOOKING TWICE;
> DEADLAND'S PARADISE,
> NOT THE KIND OF PLACE TO SAVE SOMEONE FROM.

Okay okay okay okay, *this* is my fave hookah bar.

**JASPER.** Hookah?! Will Agnes be in there?

**GRETCHEN.** Well, every ghoul who's any ghoul chills out here…

> *(At the hookah bar.)*

> *(They enter a club;* **GRETCHEN** *goes up to the* **BARTENDER***.)*

**BARTENDER.** Gretch! Baby!

**GRETCHEN.**
> MAKES NO DIFFERENCE HOW YOU FED THE WORMS,
> IT'S A SCREAM ONCE YOU ARRIVE.

> *(***JASPER** *sets about talking to* **BARTENDER***.)*

**HOOKAH SMOKERS.**
> YOU'LL BE SCREAMING,
> OOH, YOU'LL BE SCREAMING

**GRETCHEN.**

SCREAM IF YOU'RE NOT ALIVE!

**HOOKAH SMOKERS.**

OOH!

| GRETCHEN. | HOOKAH SMOKERS. |
|---|---|
| ONCE YOU GIVE YOUR GHOST, | GIVE YOUR GHOST, |
| WE ALL GIVE A TOAST. | |

**HOOKAH SMOKERS.**

TO JASPER!

**GRETCHEN.**

JASPER, JOIN IN OUR ANGELIC JIVE!

**HOOKAH SMOKERS.**

JOIN IN OUR ANGELIC –
LA LA LA LA LA LA LA LA!
JOIN IN OUR ANGELIC JIVE!

**BARTENDER.** Sorry bro, never met an "Agnes."

**GRETCHEN.** *(Comforting him, they're leaving.)*

LOOK, WE'LL WRITHE AROUND THE TOWN…

*(**BARTENDER** runs after them.)*

**BARTENDER.** Hey – livin' kid, try the arcade. That's where all the dead kids hang…

**GRETCHEN.**

'CAUSE YOUR FRIEND MAY STILL BE FOUND!

*(They go to the arcade.)*

**GRETCHEN.**

'CAUSE SHE'S GOT NOTHIN' LEFT
BUT HER SOUL AND A BAG.

| GRETCHEN. | CLUBBERS. |
|---|---|
| NOW, SHE'S LIVING DEAD. | DEAD, DEAD |

**GRETCHEN.**

SINCE HER COIL'S SPRUNG,
AND HER BUCKET'S BEEN KICKIN',
SHE'S GOT NOTHIN' TO LOSE
NOW HER TIME'S FINISHED TICKIN',
LIVING.

**GRETCHEN & CLUBBERS.**

DA-DA-DA-DEAD, DEAD.

**GRETCHEN.**

LIVING DEAD.

    (**KIDS** *playing a game similar to "Dance Dance Revolution."*)

**SHADY.** You. Boy. Pretty face. Tight jeans. If anyone can help you locate your friend, Boss Rhadamanthus can. That is, if, *if* you can beat him at the game of strength. Back room. Come.

**CLUBBERS.**

DEAD, DEAD, DEAD, DEAD
DEAD, DEAD, DEAD, DEAD.

    *(Outside in the alley people are playing craps.)*

**BOSS RHADAMANTHUS.** Now we are wrestling with arms! Best two out of three.

**JASPER.** I can't touch him, or ya know, DING!

**GRETCHEN.** I better take this.

    (**GRETCHEN** *arm wrestles.*)

CARVE A FLAT LINE THROUGH YOUR MISERIES,
AND DON'T BE FOOLED BY ALL THE GREY:

**CITIZENS.**

DON'T BE FOOLED,
DON'TCHA BE FOOLED

**GRETCHEN.**

IT'S A SCARY AWESOME STAY.

**CITIZENS.**

IT'S A SCARY STAY.

| **GRETCHEN.** | **CITIZENS.** |
|---|---|
| THERE'S NO SPLITTING HAIRS, | HOO-HOO LA, |
| ALL YOUR LIFE'S DESPAIRS | HOO-HOO LA! |
| WILL AT LAST FAST PASS AWAY. | LAST FAST PASS AWAY! |

    (**GRETCHEN** *wins!*)

**GRETCHEN & CITIZENS.**

    LA LA LA LA LA LA LA LA LA

**BOSS RHADAMANTHUS.** Okay, Okay I saw that hat on a girl at Club Helheim. She was all decked out for an Osiris concert… Had this gnarly cool bracelet…

**GRETCHEN.** *(Competitively.)* Was she pretty?

**BOSS RHADAMANTHUS.** Pretty? Not quite so pretty as you. And more sad.

**JASPER.** Club Helheim…

    IT'S JUST A ROLL AROUND THIS GRAVE…

**CHORUS.**

    OOH

**GRETCHEN.**

    WHERE YOUR

**GRETCHEN & CHORUS.**

    FRIEND IS YOURS TO SAVE.

**ANNOUNCER.** *(Voice-over.)* Welcome to the stage… Osiris!

    *(A dance floor facing a rock band.* **CLUBBERS** *cheers.)*

**OSIRIS.**

    AND THERE'S A PULSE THAT BEATS
    WHEN YOU'RE NO LONGER BREATHIN':

| **OSIRIS.** | **CLUBBERS.** |
|---|---|
| PEOPLE LIVING DEAD. | OOH… |
| GOT HER DAISIES PUSHED | LIVING DEAD… |
| FOR THE FARM THAT SHE'S BUYIN' | FARM THAT SHE'S BUYIN' |
| 'CAUSE YOU GOT NOTHIN' BUT TIME | NOTHIN' BUT TIME |
| WHEN YOU'VE NO TIME FOR DYIN'. | NO TIME FOR DYIN'. |

| **OSIRIS & GRETCHEN.** | **CLUBBERS.** |
|---|---|
| LIVING DEAD! | DA-DA-DA-DEAD, DEAD. |
| LIVING DEAD! | |

**GRETCHEN.**

    AND HE HOPES DESPITE
        DESPAIR,
    BUT IT'S HIM WHO NEEDS
        A PRAYER…
    'CAUSE HE'S GOT NOTHIN'
        LEFT
    BUT HIS SOUL AND A MAP.
    WALKING WITH THE DEAD.

**JASPER.** *(To various people.)*
I have a missing person.

Has anyone seen an Agnes Fairchild?

Excuse me, but have you seen Agnes Fairchild?

**GRETCHEN.**

    HE'S SO COOL, HE'S SO TOUGH,
    HE'D BET HIS LIFE ON TOMORROW,
    BUT DOESN'T HE KNOW LIFE
    IS NOTHING BUT SORROW?

**JASPER.** Her bracelet.

**GRETCHEN.** Come on, dance with me.

**JASPER.** I can't. I'm sorry.

**GRETCHEN.**

    LIVING…
    FORGET LIVING.
    WHO NEEDS LIVING?
    YEAH, WHO NEEDS LIVING
    WHEN YOU'RE LIVING
    DEAD?!

**CITIZENS (WOMEN).**

    SHE'S GOT
        NOTHIN' LEFT
    BUT HER SOUL
        AND A BAG.
    NOW, SHE'S
        LIVING DEAD.

**CITIZEN.**

NOTHIN' LEFT

BUT HER SOUL
    AND A BAG.
NOTHIN' LEFT

**CITIZENS (MEN).**

    CAN'T LOSE

    NOTHIN', NO
        YOU
    CAN'T LOSE

    NOTHIN', NO
        YOU

**CITIZEN.**

    BUT HER SOUL AND A BAG.

| CITIZENS (WOMEN). | CITIZEN. | CITIZENS (MEN). |
|---|---|---|
| SINCE HER COIL'S SPRUNG, | NOTHIN' LEFT | CAN'T LOST |
| AND HER BUCKET'S BEEN KICKIN', | BUT HER SOUL AND A BAG. | NOTHIN'. |

**CITIZENS (WOMEN).**

SHE'S GOT NOTHIN' TO LOSE
NOW HER TIME'S FINISHED TICKIN'

*(The* **CITIZENS** *assemble in a parade, led by* **GRETCHEN** *as grand marshal.)*

**ALL.**

AND THERE'S A PULSE THAT BEATS
WHEN YOU'RE NO LONGER BREATHIN':
PEOPLE LIVING DEAD. LIVING DEAD
GOT OUR DAISIES PUSHED
FOR THE FARM THAT WE'RE BUYIN'
'CAUSE WE GOT NOTHIN' BUT TIME
NOW WE'VE NO TIME FOR DYIN',
LIVING DEAD!
LIVING DEAD!
LIVING

**CITIZENS.**

DEAD, DEAD, DEAD, DEAD

| GRETCHEN. | CITIZENS. |
|---|---|
| IT'S THE DAY, | DEAD, DEAD, DEAD, DEAD |
| IT'S THE NIGHT, | DEAD, DEAD, DEAD, DEAD |
| IT'S THE DAWN | DEAD, DEAD, DEAD, DEAD |
| OF THE | |
| DEAD! | DEAD! |

*(As they finish the number, a bright, harsh light comes on like it's the end of the night at a club. Everyone groans, putting their hands up to their eyes and slowly exiting, except for* **JASPER** *and* **GRETCHEN***.)*

*(As the kids exit behind* **JASPER** *and* **GRETCHEN***, we reveal* **VIRGIL***, who was also at the club.)*

JASPER. Great. Just great. I spent the whole time looking for my friend and all you did was party.

GRETCHEN. Look, this is how I roll. It's what I do to keep from going crazy. All right? Don't worry. We'll find her.

VIRGIL. Hey kid!

JASPER. Virgil! What are you doing here?

VIRGIL. Hey, I've been looking for you everywhere. I got some information on your girlfriend, Agnes.

JASPER. Where is she? You find her?

VIRGIL. I got some bad news. Her soul has been marked to move on to Elysium.

GRETCHEN. Oh, no.

JASPER. Elysium?

GRETCHEN. It's where souls go…to rest for eternity.

JASPER. But, this is all a mistake! We're not supposed to be here. She's still alive!

VIRGIL. That's the thing, kid. She is dead.

JASPER. What?

VIRGIL. She died. Drowned in that lake. Here… It's her Death Manifest…

(VIRGIL *hands him a piece of paper.*)

JASPER. If she's dead then why am I here?

VIRGIL. I wish I knew, kid… The good news is that Mister Lethe has issued you a free pass through the river and back to the living world. But, you have to take it now, kid. It is a "one-time-only" pass.

JASPER. I can't. I can't just leave her…

VIRGIL. You know, you remind me of someone. He was a "Half-Life." …Traveled through the underworld like yourself. Dante. You may have heard of him. Go find Beatrix Portinari, she can help you. Goodbye, Jasper. Goodbye.

GRETCHEN. (*Sitting with him.*) I'm so sorry.

### *[MUSIC NO. 11 "HEL 'N LOKI #1"]*

*(Loud booming drums sound in the distance.)*

**JASPER.** What's that?

**GRETCHEN.** I…don't…know…

*(Two lethe goons/norse gods,* **LOKI** *and* **HEL,** *spot* **JASPER** *and* **GRETCHEN.**)

**LOKI.**

I AM LOKI!

**HEL.**

I AM HEL!

**LOKI & HEL.**

WE ARE NORSE GODS!

SEIZE THE BOY!

**GRETCHEN.** WAIT! Hel and Loki, right? I didn't catch your last name…

**LOKI.** Last name? Why it's Farfensharpinorpincleptopee pinshorpinmorganfreemanendqvist.

*(***GRETCHEN** *and* **JASPER** *sneak off.)*

**HEL.** But we go by Larsen.

*(She looks back to see that* **AGNES** *and* **JASPER** *are gone.)*

Fazza… Where did they go?

**LOKI.** Come, Hel!

### Scene Seven: The Sewers

***[MUSIC NO. 12 "THE SEWER"]***

*(In the Sewer, the River Lethe runs through.)*

**JASPER.** Where are we?

**GRETCHEN.** The Sewers. Are you all right?

*(She lights a match.)*

**JASPER.** Yeah. Look, we have to get to Elysium.

**GRETCHEN.** Listen! You don't want to mess around with those things –

**JASPER.** I *have* to find her.

**RIVER LETHE.**

   FIND HER... FIND HER... FIND HER...

**JASPER.** Oh, not this again.

**GRETCHEN.** I am telling you, you are in danger.

**JASPER.** And I am telling you that I have to find Agnes before more pictures come down...and I forget it all.

**RIVER LETHE.**

   AGNES... AGNES... AGNES...

**JASPER.** What's happening?

**RIVER LETHE.**

   PERFECT NIGHT... PERFECT NIGHT... PERFECT NIGHT...

**GRETCHEN.** I don't know the river's never done this before.

**RIVER LETHE.**

   YOU CAN'T LEAVE... YOU CAN'T LEAVE... YOU CAN'T LEAVE...

**JASPER.** *(Stamping the water.)* STOP! STOP IT!

*(The water becomes silent.)*

**GRETCHEN.** Wow... Were those your memories?

**JASPER.** Yes...

**GRETCHEN.** What happened?

**JASPER.** How do we get out of the city?

**GRETCHEN.** It's not that easy.

*(Then.)*

The only way out is through the back entrance, which is guarded by a demon called Ammut, and she's impossible to get past. You can only get through when you're called to go on to Elysium. If you try to get past her too early, *she eats your heart!*

JASPER. Look, I just tamed a ginormous three-headed dog and I outran a couple of Norse Gods, I think I can deal with one demon.

GRETCHEN. Oooh. Mister "Big Pants" now…

JASPER. Look, we get past this demon thingy and then what… Elysium?

GRETCHEN. Sure…but what are you going to do when you find Agnes? She can't go back.

JASPER. I know it's been done. That guy, Orpheus, he was alive, just like me, and he came down here to take back…take back…

GRETCHEN. You mean, Eurydice?

JASPER. Yeah. Her…

GRETCHEN. There's only one problem with the whole Orpheus scenario… Orpheus loved Eurydice…

*(Then.)*

So…if you don't love Agnes then how –

JASPER. I'll find a way around that.

*(Then.)*

GRETCHEN. Hm. Just think, if you're successful – which I highly doubt – you and your "friend" will be back in the living world and eatin' at Chuck E. Cheese…

*(Remembering.)*

Wait. Wow. Chuck E. Cheese… I think I had my birthday party there when I was a kid… Isn't that nuts? Being around you I'm starting to remember things from my life.

**JASPER.** And I've almost forgotten everything.

No point in you getting mixed up in all this, it's dangerous... So, just point me in the right direction and I'll go. Thank you for everything...

**GRETCHEN.** You sure you don't want me to come? 'Cause this shit is real and it's scary and your soul could get like lost for eternity outside those gates –

**JASPER.** I can do it. Are you gonna be okay?

**GRETCHEN.** Of course! This is my home. I've got a job... I'm in the Oprah Book Club...

**JASPER.** *OPRAH'S DEAD?!*

**GRETCHEN.** No! Don't be silly. She just transcends time and space.

> *(Then.)*

Anyway this is *your* quest, Mr. Jasper.

**JASPER.** Thanks, Gretchen.

**GRETCHEN.** You're welcome – Good luck to ya. Now, go slay a demon.

> *(He exits.)*

### *[MUSIC NO. 13 "THE FORGETTING – REPRISE"]*

YOU'RE JUST ONE MORE PERSON
I'LL SOON COME TO FORGET.
SO WHAT, YOU'VE STIRRED MY SOUL?
IN YOUR LIFE, I'VE PLAYED MY ROLE,
AND SO...

Had to get mixed up with a live guy, couldn't stick to my own kind... Dammit...

### *[MUSIC NO. 13A "SLAY A DEMON"]*

> *(**JASPER** nods as lights shift. The rest of the **COMPANY** enters. **JASPER** and **GRETCHEN** make their way through the bodies.)*

**SCREAMING MAN.** Ahh! Ahh! Don't go in there! Ahh!

## Scene Eight: Ammut's Gate

*(Guarding a small gate leaving the City, Egyptian demoness **AMMUT** – who bears a crocodile's head, a leopard's torso, and hippo's legs – is at her booth, wading in a shallow, one-person blow-up pool. She's stuffed into a civil servant's uniform, her name embroidered on the chest pocket, reading a trashy magazine. **GRETCHEN** and **JASPER** hesitantly step up. **AMMUT** is totally disinterested in the following:)*

**AMMUT.** Hello welcome to the Gates of Deadland where the Inner Circles are forbidden how can I help you.

**JASPER.** Yes. I'm trying to get to Elysium. I was wondering if you could let me through.

**AMMUT.** Let you through? What do I look like?

**JASPER.** Uh…

**AMMUT.** Well my name is "Ammut" like Dammit.

*(Indicating her body, getting slightly interested.)*

And all this? Makes me a hundered percent Egyptian demoness. Baby, I was born with the lips of a crocodile… the luscious rosette coat of a leopard…and the butt of a hippopotamus. You just gotta love yourself, you know baby.

*(Then.)*

Get through? When all this…

*(Referring to Hell.)*

Freezes over.

**JASPER.** Look, I'm "alive" and I need help getting back to the Living World! So are you going to let me through or what?

**AMMUT.** Baby, that's my gate, and I make sure nobody gets through it unless they have purged their soul of their life's GREATEST MISDEED! That's right – they gotta tell Mama Ammut what weighs down their heart like a stone on a feather! Now, where's my Blind Justice?!

(*Out come three sexy chorus girls as* **BLIND JUSTICE**, *each holding a golden balancing scale.*)

### [MUSIC NO. 14 "HUNGRY FOR YOUR HEART"]

**AMMUT**. Now for every confession, the heart becomes a little lighter. AND if a person can confess the one thing in their life *they regret the most!* – They'll find their heart soon weighs practically nothin'. And, then, and only then, may a person pass through my gate and out of the City. But if you can't... I eat your heart, baby. (*An obnoxiously loud laugh.*) HAH-HAH-HAH!
BABY, YOU CREPT TO MY BOOTH,
PRAYIN' MAYBE, I WON'T GIT TO THE TRUTH
BUT LAWD, I'VE LIVED A LONG TIME,
AND I'VE WALLOWED IN YOUR MUD.
LAWD, I'VE LIVED A LONG TIME,
AND I CAN SMELL YOUR TYPE OF BLOOD.

(**JASPER** *considers. Then pushes* **GRETCHEN** *back, desperately.*)

I'm gonna need some back-up!

**JASPER**. So, uh, how do we do this whole "weighing my heart thing?"

(**AMMUT** *reaches into his chest and pulls out his heart and throws it on the scale.* **GRETCHEN** *enters.*)

**GRETCHEN**. Wait! He's not dead!

**JASPER**. Dying...

**GRETCHEN**. We gotta get you a new heart.

**JASPER**. Gretchen.

(*Thinks of her own.*)

**GRETCHEN**. Here take mine.

(*She pulls out her own heart and plunges it into* **JASPER**; *he bursts with a shot of adrenaline.*)

**JASPER**. GAAAASP! Thank you.

**GRETCHEN**. There. I knew you needed me!

**JASPER**. *(To **AMMUT**.)* I'm ready!

| **AMMUT**. | **BLIND JUSTICE**. |
|---|---|
| WOAH! | WOAH! |
| CRUEL BOY: YOU'VE RUINED JUNGLES OF GIRLS. | CRUEL BOY, THUMP THUMP-UH, THUMP, THUMP |
| BUT, I'M NO FOOL, BOY: | FOOL BOY, THUMP |
| YOU TOSS THE OYSTERS FOR PEARLS. | THUMP-UH, THUMP, THUMP |
| LAWD, I'VE LIVED A LONG TIME, | THUMP-UH, THUMP-UH |
| AND I'VE MET ME SOME MIS'RABLE MEN! | THOSE MIS'RABLE, THUMP |
| BUT LAWD, FROM NOW TO ALL TIME, | THUMP-UH THUMP-UH |
| I'LL CHOOSE YOUR KIND AGAIN AND AGAIN. | AGAIN. |
| I LOVE A | |
| BAD KID! (GIVE A TASTE! I WAN' A LITTLE!) | BAD KID! OOO. BAD KID! |
| BAD KID! (DRESS YOU UP, AND HAVE A SLICE.) | OOO… HAVE A SLICE. |
| FROM YOUR NECK TO YOUR BUTT, | OOH… |
| I WANNA CUT DOWN THE MIDDLE, | CUT DOWN THE MIDDLE |
| WITH A WHITTLE AT THE GUT, TELL YOU WHAT: OOH, TELL YOU WHAT | TELL YOU WHAT: OOH, TELL YOU WHAT |
| DON'T THAT SOUND NICE? | |

| **AMMUT**. | **BLIND JUSTICE**. |
|---|---|
| I'M HUNGRY FOR YOUR HEART, | THUMP THUMP THUMP, OOH |
| | I GOT A CRAVIN'! |
| YAS, I'M HUNGRY FOR YOUR HEART, | THUMP THUMP THUMP, OOH |

| | I GOT A CRAVIN'! |
| HAH-HAH! YOU'RE DANGER, | THUMP-UH THUMP-UH |
| BOUND TO BREAK ALL MY | THUMP-UH THUMP-UH |
| LAWS. | |
| GAME-CHANGER, YOU'RE WHY | THUMP-UH THUMP-UH |
| GOD GAVE ME CLAWS. | GOD GAVE ME CLAWS. |
| 'CAUSE LAWD, IT'S BEEN A | LAWD! THUMP |
| LONG TIME… | THUMP-UH |
| YOU'RE ONLY HUMAN, AFTER | THUMP-UH THUMP-UH |
| ALL. | |
| SO LAWD, FOR NOW AND ALL | LAWD! THUMP |
| TIME | THUMP-UH |
| WHEN YOU SCREAM I'M | |
| GONNA ANSWER | |
| THE CALL. | THE CALL! |
| SO BE BAD KID. MY INSIDE'S | BAD KID! |
| ALL HOOTS AND HOWLS. | OOH… BAD KID |
| IT'S | |
| BAD, KID. NEED TO GET YOU | BAD! OOH… DOUSED IN |
| DOUSED IN GREASE, | GREASE |
| PINCH SOME CUMIN, | OOH |
| CAYENNE, | |
| SO YOU KICK PAST MY JOWLS, | KICK PAST MY JOWLS |
| TO MAH BOWELS, BABY THEN: | OOH |
| SAY AMEN! LET'S HAVE A | HALLELUJAH! |
| PIECE! | |
| I'M HUNGRY FOR YOUR | THUMP THUMP THUMP, |
| HEART, | OOH |
| | I GOT A CRAVIN'! |

| **AMMUT.** | **BLIND JUSTICE.** |
| YAS! SO HUNGRY FOR YOUR | THUMP THUMP THUMP, |
| HEART, BABY, BABY | OOH |
| | I GOT A CRAVIN'! |
| HUNGRY FOR YOUR HEART | HUNGRY FOR YOUR |
| | HEART, WOAH! |

HUNGRY FOR YOUR HEART HUNGRY FOR YOUR
HEART, WOAH!

**AMMUT.**
BABY, Y'KNOW I CRAVE YOU,
SO NOW I THINK I'LL ENSLAVE YOU.

**AMMUT.** **BLIND JUSTICE.**
I'M OH SO HUNGRY FOR THU-UM PAH!
YOUR HEART!
YOW! THUMP.

*(Then.)*

Bear your soul, Baby! Tell me your biggest REGRET, your biggest MISDEED – And if your sexy tight ass can't do that...then I take the cake!

**JASPER.** All right! I'm shy and awkward around others... I ignore my friends...

*(As **JASPER** speaks, the scale becomes lighter, lighter, lighter...)*

**AMMUT.** More! More!

**JASPER.** I don't work hard enough at school. I got kicked off the swim team!

**AMMUT.** Nothin'!

**JASPER.** I didn't hide my father's pills when he got out of rehab.

**AMMUT.** Now, we're gettin' somewhere!

**JASPER.** Maybe I wasn't a good enough son to my mother... Maybe that's why she left! Maybe that's why she chose her boyfriend Todd over me!

*(All goes still...but –)*

**GRETCHEN.** Jasper...your heart is still heavier than the feather.

**AMMUT.**
HAH-HAH-HAH!

I SWORE MY BONES YOU'D BE TOUGH,
OFF THE CUFF BUT COMMITTED.
BUT YOU BIT IT. THAT WAS ROUGH.

AIN'T ENOUGH! SO SORRY, CHUMP!

**BLIND JUSTICE.**

HUNGRY FOR YOUR HEART, OH WAH!

**JASPER.** Wait! It's my fault! Agnes is dead because of me! I wasn't there for her when she needed me.

(**JASPER**'s *heart, now weightless, floats up in the air.* **AMMUT** *grabs it.*)

**AMMUT.** NOOOOOOOOOO!

**GRETCHEN.** Jasper, you did it! You can enter the gates!

**AMMUT.** Well. Too bad I'm a sore loser, baby.

(**AMMUT** *crushes his heart.*)

Come on ladies, I'm still hungry! Let's go order me some Moo Goo Gai Pan.

**JASPER.** Oh shit! That was my heart!

**GRETCHEN.** Keep mine. I don't need it. We have to go Jasper.

**JASPER.** *Temos que ir!* (We have to go!) Oh no! *Espere! Estou falando Português?* (Wait! Am I speaking Portuguese?)

**GRETCHEN.** Shit! Phase Three!

### *[MUSIC NO. 15 "HEL 'N LOKI #2"]*

**JASPER.** *Temos de nos apressar!* (We have to hurry!)

(*Suddenly, we see* **LOKI** *and* **HEL** *appear, and they throw their lightning bolts at* **JASPER** *and* **GRETCHEN**.)

**LOKI.**

I AM LOKI!

**HEL.**

I AM HEL!

**LOKI & HEL.**

WE'RE STILL NORSE GODS!

**LOKI.**

WE CARRY BOLTS OF

LIGHTNING THAT ARE
SAID TO BE QUITE HARMFUL!

**HEL.**

WE CONJURE CUMULUS CLOUDS –

**LOKI & HEL.**

YES!

**HEL.**

SOMETIMES BY THE ARM FULL!

**LOKI.**

OUR ABS ARE RIPPED AND
AS SUCH THEY'RE THE
ENVY OF KING MIDAS!

**HEL.**

PLUS WE HAVE HUGE
INCISORS WITH NO
SIGN OF PERIODONTITIS!

**LOKI & HEL.**

SEIZE THE BOY!

**GRETCHEN.** RUN!

*(Actors ad lib.)*

**HEL.** Hurry Fajah!

**LOKI.** I'm moving at lightning speed.

## Scene Nine: Lethe's Office

*(On a soundstage,* **MR. LETHE** *sits pretentiously in a director's chair à la Cecil B. Demille. He is mid-interruption with* **ASSISTANT HATHAWAY**. *Nearby, Actors prepare.)*

**MR. LETHE.** Lapinski, it's Lethe, I'm at the commercial shoot. I need you to move four hundred thousand units. Don't worry I've got "Near Deaths" arriving every day. Product in Chicago in two days. Don't worry I have Amazon Prime.

**HATHAWAY.** Chief, sorry to interrupt your shoot…

**MR. LETHE.** What is it?

**HATHAWAY.** The boy has exited the gates.

**MR. LETHE.** WHAT? HOW?

**HATHAWAY.** We faked the manifest to Elysium like you said, AND we gave the boy a pass through the river; but he didn't want to leave Deadland. He decided to go after her instead. He beat Ammut.

*(Under her breath.)*

That bitch…

**MR. LETHE.** I am grumpy.

**HATHAWAY.** Here, have some water…

**LETHE.** Are you nuts?! I can't drink that! That's the big secret of Deadland: It's the water that makes you forget!

**HATHAWAY.** Sorry… I forgot…

**LETHE.** Where is he now?

**HATHAWAY.** Hel and Loki were in hot pursuit, but now that the live one and the girl are outside the gates, they'll be impossible to find.

**MR. LETHE.** Hmmmm… This boy is actually starting to impress me… He may be the one thing I've been waiting for. Find him! This is all going according to plan, Hathaway! First, I'll overthrow those nimrods Neptune and Jupiter and then I'm comin' for you,

Pluto… Oh, yes, your days are finally numbered! You stuck me with a river in Hell? I'll do you one worse! How's Cleveland, sound? Now, let's continue on with the next commercial. I'm looking for happy but not saccharin. I want BROADWAY but not Broadway. I want girl next door but two doors down. Do you understand? Action!

*[MUSIC NO. 16 "THE COMMERCIAL"]*

**LETHE'S GIRL #1**. *(Overly sympathetic, like a commercial for yeast infections.)* Have you been around a Living Person for too long?

**LETHE'S GIRL #2**. Are you having "Near-Life Experiences?"

**MR. LETHE**. *(An incredibly awkward read; terrible on-camera actor.)* Oh hi there. Then be hydrated! Ninety-eight percent of those who drink a twelve ounce bottle of Lethe brand water, say they felt better in no time.

**HATHAWAY**. *(An incredibly fast disclaimer.)* Drink Lethe water responsibly. Side effects may include: burping, yodeling, involuntary snapping, jiggly leg, jazz hands, cat fights, scratchy sweater, and sausage fingers.

**LETHE**. Lethe brand water. Remember…

**ALL**.

LETHE IS MORE!

## Scene Ten: The Great Gulf

***[MUSIC NO. 16A "THE GREAT GULF"]***

(**GRETCHEN** *and* **JASPER** *emerge in a new, wooded area, where they find a gaping chasm before them. There's a yellow traffic sign.*)

**JASPER.** *Fico feliz em ficar longe deles.* [I'm glad we got away from them.] Oh, God…

**GRETCHEN.** You did good back there, live boy. It was impressive.

**JASPER.** You too. Thanks for saving me.

**GRETCHEN.** It's the least I could do.

**JASPER.** Holy crap! The pit…! Where are we?

**GRETCHEN.** We've reached the Great Gulf. It's a deep chasm, and if you fall into it, you'll end up in the Wasteland, where your soul could be lost for eternity… Gotta be some kind of bridge, or a connection at some point…

**JASPER.** You think they positioned a three-headed canine and a heart-eating demon at the exits of the other circles, but then here, they built a bridge?

**GRETCHEN.** I mean, maybe it's like, "Surprise! It's easy." …No?

**JASPER.** The sign. It's a riddle…

**GRETCHEN.** "To cross the gap, there is no map,
No chance to bridge the parts."

**JASPER.** "The way to pass, is clear as glass:
The meeting of two hearts."

**GRETCHEN.** I don't know what it means.

**JASPER.** My head. Here, give me the water…

(*He drinks.*)

*Molto bene.* [Very good.] …And what's your name again?

(*Then.*)

This has got to stop!

GRETCHEN. Just keep drinking the water.

(*Then.*)

JASPER. All the pictures are almost gone… It's all becoming so cloudy. The cliff, the water, that day…

(*He downs it, but it's empty.*)

There's one picture left, but I can't barely see her. It's the night before… We are on her couch, talking about *Star Trek*. It's the beginning of everything… I told her about the swimming pool. "Let's be the first to feel something real" …I can still see it… It's the last picture on the wall… Me and Agnes… I was happy with her, wasn't I? I lose this and she'll be gone forever…

(*There's a beat.*)

GRETCHEN. Wow.

JASPER. What?

GRETCHEN. I just have never had anyone feel about me the way you feel about Agnes.

JASPER. Come with me and maybe I can get you home. Back to the Living World, your life…

GRETCHEN. People who are dead don't get to go back…

JASPER. You don't believe that… There must have been a reason why you came with me…

GRETCHEN. No… Unfortunately, I came with you for other reasons… Stupid me.

(*Starts to go.*)

JASPER. Where are you going?

GRETCHEN. Back to my "non-life."

JASPER. Wait! There has to be a reason why I'm here!

(*She comes back at him.*)

GRETCHEN. You're so naive… You wanna be like Orpheus… but, you know what? Orpheus failed. Just like you will…

(*She starts to go.*)

JASPER. As long as we *don't look back*… We won't fail…

### [MUSIC NO. 17 "STROKE BY STROKE"]

**JASPER.**

DON'T YOU KNOW THE WORLD IS WATER?
YOU CAN'T JUST FLOAT ON IT.
CAN'T SKIM IT,
AFRAID TO SWIM IT.
NO, YOU CAN'T JUST STAY ON LAND.

SOMEHOW, YOU GOTTA BREAK THAT WATER,
KICK AND PULL THROUGH IT.
YOU CROSS EACH LENGTH
WITH STRIDE AND STRENGTH,
YOU PACE THE COURSE
WITH EVEN FORCE,
YOUR HAND IN FRONT OF HAND,

YOU GO
STROKE BY STROKE BY STROKE BY STROKE BY STROKE.
YOU GO
STROKE BY STROKE BY STROKE BY STROKE BY STROKE.

SO MEET ME AT THE TOUCH OF WATER –
AND TAKE SOME LAPS WITH ME.
SOME FREE, SOME TEST,
WITH OUR BACK AND BREAST,
WE'LL KEEP OUR STYLE
FOR THE MILLIONTH MILE,

AND WHEN IT'S MORE THAN WE CAN STAND,
WE'LL GO
STROKE BY STROKE BY STROKE BY STROKE BY STROKE.
WE'LL GO
STROKE BY STROKE BY STROKE BY STROKE BY STROKE.

> (**JASPER** *walks to the edge of the Gulf, peering over;*
> **GRETCHEN** *stands back.*)

LET OTHERS WALK AROUND AN OCEAN,
LET OTHERS TRY TO BUILD A BRIDGE ACROSS.
BUT YOU AND ME, WE FALL IN, FALL IN,
NEVER SURE WE'LL SURVIVE.
BUT WE'LL FIND OUT HOW DEEP,

LEARN THE SECRETS THEY KEEP
AT THE BOTTOM WHERE WE ARRIVE.
NOW, LET'S JUMP.

**GRETCHEN**. What? No.

**JASPER.**

LET'S JUMP!

**GRETCHEN.**

Jasper, you *can't*.

**JASPER.**

WE'LL NEVER KNOW WE'RE ALIVE
TILL WE JUMP, TILL WE DIVE…!

> (**JASPER** *closes his eyes, and steps one foot forward into the Gulf…*)

**GRETCHEN.**

Jasper! I'm serious!

> (*…And discovers the "chasm" is merely illusion: a glass floor connects the two sides.*)

**JASPER.**

AND WE'LL GO
STROKE BY STROKE BY STROKE BY STROKE BY STROKE!
WE'LL GO
STROKE BY STROKE BY STROKE BY STROKE BY STROKE
BY STROKE!

> (*Then.*)

…It's a glass bridge. The Gulf is just an illusion!

> (**JASPER** *stands in mid-air, extending his hand to* **GRETCHEN** *on land.*)

SO MEET ME AT THE TOUCH OF WATER –
AND TAKE THE SWIM WITH ME…

Take my hand.

**GRETCHEN**. I can't. You know what happens if we fall –

**JASPER**. Trust me.

*(Beat; She turns and takes a deep breath.* **JASPER** *extends his hand to her, and she takes it – Ding! The world stops.)*

**[MUSIC NO. 18 "THE REMEMBERING"]**

**DARYL.** Hey Agnes, you wanna meet in the locker room after Spanish class?

**GRAHAM.** Agnes, I don't want you to see this Jasper anymore.

**JASPER.** Agnes, you're the most amazing person I've ever known.

*(Silence.)*

*(Lights shift back to* **AGNES/GRETCHEN** *with* **JASPER**, *suspended in mid-air.)*

**AGNES.** Jasper – Jasper – I – It's me!
AGNES IS – ME!
*AGNES WAS ALWAYS ME!*

**(JASPER** *seems confused, disoriented.)*

**JASPER.** What?

**AGNES.** Jasper!

*(She embraces him tightly.)*

I had forgotten you, I had forgotten all of it… But you – you did it…you came back for me! I knew you felt the same for me as I do for you! I knew you loved me! That's what the riddle means.

**(JASPER** *doesn't seem to recognize what she's saying.)*

**JASPER.** I'm sorry. I don't love you.

*(Crack. The glass.)*

**AGNES.** What…? Jasper, don't move, the glass is cracking!

*(Crack crack crack.)*

**JASPER.** Jasper… Who's Jasper?

*(The glass beneath their feet shatters, and they fall into the Great Gulf.)*

**COMPANY.**
BYE! GOODBYE!
GOODBYE! GOODBYE!
GOODBYE! GOODBYE!
GOODBYE! GOODBYE! YUH!
JASPER, GOODBYE!

## End of Act I

# ACT II

## Scene One: A memory

*(An entr'acte. Lights up on* **JASPER** *and* **AGNES**.*)*

*(In a memory.)*

### *[MUSIC NO. 19 "OPENING ACT II"]*

**GRETCHEN AS AGNES.** The new *Star Trek*s are great, but the old ones. I mean *Wrath of Kahn*!

**JASPER.** I know!

**JASPER & AGNES.** Kahn!

**AGNES.** *(In a thick Scottish accent.)* I can't do it Captain, I don't have the power.

**JASPER.** *(In the style of Dr. McCoy.)* Dammit Jim, I'm just a country doctor!

**AGNES.** I always cry like a baby when Spock dies, saving the whole ship and running into that reactor. Sacrificing himself.

**JASPER.** Yeah, that's crazy.

**AGNES.** No, it's noble.

**JASPER.** I guess you've got to be a Vulcan.

**AGNES.** You forget, he's half human.

**JASPER.** Yeah…but nobody does something like that.

**AGNES.** Sure they do…

**JASPER.** Only in movies and video games… People…are mostly disappointing…

**AGNES.** Jasper –

**JASPER.** It doesn't seem real. My mother cheating on my father… It seems like the most unreal thing that could ever happen; but it happens every day. Parents don't stay together. I'm sorry, I know you don't want to hear all my shit –

**AGNES.** It's okay. We've been friends for a long time... I have to ask you, how come we've never...

**JASPER.** Never what...?

**AGNES.** You know...

**JASPER.** Um...well... I don't know...

> *(Then.)*

I do remember the swimming pool at the Y when we were thirteen... There were only a few of us in the pool, but you took your bikini bottoms off underwater... You were swimming naked... And nobody knew... Except me –

**AGNES.** Because you had those giant goggles... Almost like deep sea diver goggles...

> *(Beat.)*

I knew you were looking...

**JASPER.** You did?

**AGNES.** I did...

**JASPER.** You were the first girl I ever saw naked... I mean, "live" – I couldn't get you out of my head... You looked perfect. You *are* perfect.

**AGNES.** You think I'm perfect? My stepmother is perfect. I don't think she's ever made a mistake in her life. Me? I am far from perfect.

### *[MUSIC NO. 20 "SOMETHING FOR REAL"]*

There are things you don't know about me, Jasper.

YOU SEE THIS HOODIE? IT MUMBLES, "AIN'T I SWEET?"
THIS HAIR DYED MELLOW YELLOW SWEARS, "I'M
    COMPLETE."
A GOODIE-GOODIE, WITH NO TRACE OF DESPAIR...
COMBED AND TUCKED,
PRIMPED AND PLUCKED.
BUT A HAND IS COV'RING MY MOUTH –
SCREAMING! – "LET THIS ARMOR BE STEEL."

I JUST WANT TO SAY
SOMETHING FOR REAL.

**JASPER.** Well, say it. What don't I know about you?

**AGNES.** Like Daryl...

**JASPER.** From Spanish class?

**AGNES.** He was my first.

**JASPER.** Why him?

**AGNES.** I guess I did it because... I didn't think you would...

**JASPER.** *(Hit hard.)* I'm sorry... I've seen first hand how it all ends up. How awful it all becomes... I'm afraid I'll do the same to you...

MOM TAKES COMMUNION, WHILE DAD TAKES ONE MORE LINE.
SHE PRAYS TO JESUS, FREEZES SMILES: "ALL IS FINE."
HE LETS THEIR UNION SHATTER, SHE TURNS HER CHEEK.
I GO ON.
GOING GONE.
BUT MY HAND GRIPS – CLENCHED TO A FIST,
POUNDING –! CAN'T THEY SEE HOW I FEEL?

I JUST WANNA DO
SOMETHING FOR REAL.

*(Then.)*

**AGNES.** Let's change things. From this moment on, we will do it right, you and me. We will be the first to make it happen. It has to start somewhere, why not tonight? When they look back and they talk about the great couples of all time, we will be up there: Romeo and Juliet, Anthony and Cleopatra, Orpheus and Eurydice...

*(He struggles.)*

AND WE WON'T
DARE LOOK BACK

*(He looks into her eyes, seeing her as if for the first time.)*

**JASPER & AGNES.**

> AND WE WON'T
> DARE LOOK BACK.

> > *(She takes off her shirt; she stands before him. He slowly takes off his shirt. He moves toward her. He reaches in to touch her face.)*

> LET'S LOSE OUR COVER. LET'S FACE THIS IN THE FLESH.
> I'M TIRED OF HIDING, STRIDING CLOSE TO THE LINE.
> WE MIGHT DISCOVER HOW A SOUL CAN REFRESH.

**JASPER.**

> NO MORE LIVING SO… DEAD.

**AGNES.**

> NO MORE DEAD – BUT ALIVE.

**JASPER & AGNES.**

> GRAB MY HAND, FRIEND; PULL ME IN TIGHT.
> TOUCHING,

**JASPER.**

> NOW WE'RE

**JASPER & AGNES.**

> READY TO DEAL

**AGNES.**

> WITH WHAT WE COULD MAKE:

**JASPER & AGNES.**

> SOMETHING FOR REAL.

**JASPER.**

> LET'S BE THE FIRST

**JASPER & AGNES.**

> SOMETHING FOR REAL.
> JASPER AND AGNES –
> SOMETHING FOR REAL.

> > *(As the song ends, they kiss and the world revolves again. The flashback ends and we are back in the Wasteland.)*

## Scene Two: The Wasteland

*(Endless desert. The deathly hot sun bears down.*
**JASPER** *is face-first in the sand.* **AGNES** *rushes to him.)*

### *[MUSIC NO. 21 "SAVING JASPER"]*

**AGNES**. Jasper! Jasper! – Damn it, we're in the Wasteland!

*(Goes to* **JASPER**.*)*

TRY TO STOP IT.
FIGHT FOR YOUR LIFE!
NEVER LOSE SIGHT OF YOUR LIFE!
YES, I KNOW WHAT I SAID,
BUT YOU FIGHT THE FORGETTING.
JUST THINK OF THE BEST THINGS,
AND FORGET WHAT'S UPSETTING,
LET THE TIME PASS AND SOMEHOW WE'LL FILL UP YOUR
   MIND
LIKE A BOAT MADE TO FLOAT, WE CAN DO IT,
WE'LL REMIND YOU OF
AGNES, YOUR BEST FRIEND,
WHOM YOU'VE FIN'LLY FOUND SOMEHOW…
I CAN'T BELIEVE YOU CAME.
JASP, YOU'RE NOT THE SAME. BUT…

*(***JASPER*** stirs, awakening from something.)*

NOW… YOU… FIGHT.

**JASPER**. Uhhh – ahhh! Help! Help! I'm with a scary girl!

**AGNES**. No! My name is Agnes and you are Jasper!

**JASPER**. I don't know Jasper and I don't know you! You're confusing me!

**AGNES**. I'm Agnes! I'm Agnes. Please say you remember me!

**JASPER**. Yeah. I think I remember…

**AGNES**. Good. Good!

**JASPER**. I'm… Daryl.

**AGNES**. No. Not Daryl.

JASPER. I'm pretty sure I'm Daryl, from Spanish class.

AGNES. Daryl is an idiot. I mean, *you're* not an idiot, Daryl is.

JASPER. But, I'm Daryl.

AGNES. AH! This is nuts.

JASPER. If you're Agnes, I think you're supposed to go out with me because I'm Daryl.

AGNES. Listen, you are Jasper and I am Agnes… And we have to get out of here –

> *(The very loud sound of an aircraft hovering somewhere in the air. It grows deafening, and* **AGNES** *and* **JASPER** *reel, preparing for its arrival. Suddenly there is a boom, clunk, crash – engine failure. In comes a very old woman with flight goggles. She is* **BEATRIX***: seven hundred and fifty years old, and she really looks it; perhaps she's withered away to a mere puppet.)*

BEATRIX. Ahhh wet myself again. God-for-crappin'-landings always make my bladder blow!

> **(BEATRIX** *pulls out an ancient cell phone, you know, one from the 80s.)*

Hello?! This is Beatrix Portinari, Elysium Transit Authority! Car needs some *RE-PAIR*, Purgatorio's taken a poop again. Yeah. Yeah… How the hell should I know, I'm somewhere in the friggin' Wasteland!

> *(She sees* **AGNES***.)*

Ahhh! Stay back!

> *(She pulls out two guns and starts shooting into the sky till she clicks, out of bullets.)*

AGNES. Wait, we're not dangerous! You're Beatrix Portinari! We've been looking for you!

BEATRIX. *(Pulling out two long jungle machetes, she does a couple of moves toward* **JASPER***, drawing the blades to his neck as though to decapitate him.)* Who the frig are yous twos?

AGNES. I'm Agnes.

**JASPER.** Daryl.

**AGNES.** No, that's not Daryl. This is Jasper, the "live boy" from the news. Can you help us?

**JASPER.** *Eu não conheço essa mulher.* [I don't know this woman.]

> (*JASPER is wandering around like a curious little child, looking at tumbleweeds, or animal skulls, scorpions, being dragged into the sand, etc.*)

**BEATRIX.** Ah, he's a "restart." Tell me somethin'…Why are you two outside the gates?

**AGNES.** We were headed to Elysium. *He* needs to go home…and…

> *(Then.)*

*I* want to go home, too.

**BEATRIX.** Only Pluto can send a dead girl back.

**AGNES.** Great! Then I'd like to go see Pluto.

**BEATRIX.** Ain't that easy! You think you can just waltz right up to Pluto and he'll just send you back? You know how many times Elvis has tried? What makes you so special?

**AGNES.** Well, in the Living World, we were…we were…

**BEATRIX.** Oh, I see. You both in love ain't ya?

**AGNES.** We had *one* night… One incredible night…

> *(Beat.)*

**BEATRIX.** It ain't worth it sweetheart. Can I tell you what we should do? I should take you both back to where you belong… Once I get Ol' Purgatorio fixed up?

**AGNES.** Purgatorio?

**BEATRIX.** My flyin' car. Yep. I'll take him on to Elysium and I'll take you back to the city.

**AGNES.** No! I can't leave him!

**BEATRIX.** This "love thing" only leads to trouble, for everybody… Take me, Beatrix Portinari. For nine years – this guy, Dante – *you may have heard of him* – he pines for me, makes me his *muse.* But, as everyone knows…I

never let him once come into my casa for a little "Bada
Bing"… 'Cause I knew, this love thing is bad news –

**JASPER.** Hola, *señoritas!* I'm Daryl.

> *(He puts his arms around* **ANGES** *and* **BEATRIX**.
> *Flashback. A sexy Italian man enters. Yep. It's*
> **DANTE ALIGHIERI**. *This flashback is slightly
> stylized as if it's a bad Italian soap opera.)*

### [MUSIC NO. 21A "DANTE: THE OPERA"]

**DANTE.**

> BEATRIX… MY LOVA…

**BEATRIX.** What? What? What? Dante? How'd you get here?

**AGNES.** How did he get here? How did *I* get here?

**JASPER.** I'm Daryl.

**DANTE.**

> OH… BEATRIX! I'VE A HAD-A TOO MUCH A DA VINO, AND I
> AM-A TORMENTED BY MY INFERNO.
> It-a keep-a me up-a all night-a. I feel like a mamaluke.
> I MUSTA ASK-A YOU FOR SOMETHING…

**BEATRIX.** My pasta fagioli?

**DANTE.** No! Not your pasta fagioli!

> IN ORDER FOR ME TO FINISH MY GREAT WORK I-A MUSTA
> GO BRAVELY INTO THE UNDERWORLD. THEREFORE I A
> MUSTA HAVEA YOUR HEART. I MUST BECOME A "HALF-
> LIFE."

**BEATRIX.** A "Half-life"?

**JASPER.** A "Half-life."

**DANTE.**

> SI! A "HALF-LIFE" IS-A SO FILLED-A WITH THE LOVE OF
> ANOTHER PERSON THAT THEY ARE-A GRANTED TWO
> WISHES IN THE UNDERWORLD… I WILL-A USE-A THOSE
> TWO WISHES TO-A TRAVEL THE INFERNO AND THEN-A
> FINISH MY GREAT WORK OF ART. I MUST-A HAVE-A YOUR-A
> HEART.

**BEATRIX.**
> YOU MUST-A HAVE-A MY HEART
> I DON'T KNOW… THIS LOVE THING ONLY LEADS TO
> > TROUBLE…

> > *(An Italian fight begins with a lot of shouting and arm gestures.)*

**DANTE.**
> TROUBLE?
> Why you gotta be like-a dis –

**BEATRIX.** *(Overlapping.)* Whatta ya mean me be like this –

**DANTE.** *(Overlapping.)* Mama said you were trouble and that
I –

**BEATRIX.** *(Overlapping.)* Oh, your Mama said I was trouble –

**DANTE.** *(Overlapping.)* Don't-a you talk-a about my mama!

**BEATRIX.** *(Overlapping.)* I love when you get angry!

> *(They make out furiously; flashback ends. **DANTE** exits.)*

My heart is friggin' yours Dante! It's all yours!

> *(**BEATRIX** is still making out with the air.)*

**AGNES.** What…?

**JASPER.** I want some Pasta fagioli.

**AGNES.** Ms. Portinari…

**BEATRIX.** All right! All right! So, we had one night! What's the big deal?

**AGNES.** Yeah, but he finished the *Inferno*, because of you!

**BEATRIX.** But, I never saw him again. He got his inspiration, finished his book and that was it. Is that what you want, dead girl? To be cast off like some worn out pair of Gucci flip-flops?

> *(Then.)*

The thing is… I loved Dante… He just didn't love me back.

**AGNES.** *(This hits her hard.)* You inspired Dante to finish a great piece of art, and what did I do for Jasper? …I got us stuck in the Underworld. Jasper doesn't love me… Not the way I love him…

> *(Then.)*

Take him on to Elysium and take me back to the city.

**BEATRIX.** Trust me dead girl, you're makin' the right choice.

> *(The sound of another hover craft entering the air space.)*

They're here*! (Looks up.)* Took 'em long enough.

**AGNES.** Dante may have had your love, but at least Jasper will always have my heart…literally.

**BEATRIX.** Ha. What's that mean?

**AGNES.** Oh, he needed it to save his life. So I put my heart inside him.

**BEATRIX.** Oh, my God. Your heart? Your actual heart?

**AGNES.** Yeah –

**BEATRIX.** Then he's just like Dante! He's a Half-life!

**JASPER.** Half-life.

**AGNES.** *(Realizing.)* That's great!

**BEATRIX.** No, it isn't! He thinks he's Daryl. He could use his two wishes at any moment and not realize what he's doing.

**JASPER.** *(As* **DARYL.***)* Hey, I have a freaky idea, let's go bang one out in my Ford Focus.

**BEATRIX.** AHHH! I'm gettin' outta here before we *all* end up in the back of his Ford Focus bein' boned up against the glass!

**AGNES.** Please! You have to take us!

**BEATRIX.** Well, I'm afraid that's gonna be more of a problem than me parallel parkin' Purgs in a packed parking lot without peein' my pants!

### [MUSIC NO. 22 "HEL 'N LOKI #3"]

*(Freaks out.)*

**BEATRIX.** I'm outta here

*(Exits.)*

**AGNES.** Jasper –

**JASPER.** Daryl –

**AGNES.** Look, I'll figure out a way to get us to Elysium! Just don't wish for anything! We have to hurry before the Norse Gods find us.

**JASPER.** That sounds awesome! I so wish I could hang with some Norse Gods!

**AGNES.** *(Realizing.)* NO! I told you not to wish for anything!

*(Suddenly,* **HEL** *and* **LOKIE** *appear.)*

**HEL & LOKI.** SEIZE THE BOY!

**LOKI.** You are coming with me!

*(***JASPER** *ad libs.)*

**HEL.** You will return with us! Now!

*(***HEL** *and* **LOKI** *grab* **AGNES**.*)*

**AGNES.** Let go! Where are you taking us?!

**HEL.** Mr. Lethe's factories.

**AGNES.** Mr. Lethe?! Factories?! *For what?!*

**HEL.** Punishment.

**AGNES.** Punishment?! For what?!

**HEL.** For being a bad, bad, bad, bad, *(Ad lib as needed: "Oh your skin is so soft what do you use? Deadland makes my skin so dry. I'm always looking for new moisturizers.")* bad girl.

## Scene Three: The Factories

***[MUSIC NO. 23 "BEAT AND BROKEN SPIRITS"]***

*(In the dark we hear:)*

**LITTLE LU.**
PUNISHED SOULS, THE GRIM CONDEMNED:
A WOEFUL LOT BE THESE.
THEY SUFFER DEATHLESS, SLAVING BREATHLESS
IN MR. LETHE'S FACTORIES!

*(Red light strobes through an endless factory warehouse. Haze obscures our view, and the sound of metal smashing against metal rings abrasively in the air. Heavy, thumping club music plays, and if it didn't all feel so hellish, it could actually be quite fun.)*

**FACTORY WORKERS.**
O, MISERY AND WOE! AND WOE!
(BEAT, BEAT, BEAT, BEAT AND BROKEN SPIRITS.)
O, MISERY AND WOE! AND WOE!
(BEAT, BEAT, BEAT, BEAT AND BROKEN SPIRITS.)

*(**LITTLE LU**, the floor supervisor, is a flannel-wearing, psychotic redneck, a relative of Leatherface, who introduces us to the miserable and tortured **FACTORY WORKERS**.)*

*(**HEL** dumps **AGNES** to the floor harshly, cuffing her body to the railing.)*

**AGNES.** Take me to Mr. Lethe *now!*

**HEL.** Oh, Mr. Lethe never come down here… This where you get your *punishment.*

**AGNES.** I haven't done anything wrong!

**LITTLE LU.** Oh, Pretty Kitty, everyone done *something* wrong…

*(Speak-sings.)*

SISYPHUS, THE CLEV'REST KING,
SOME SAY TOO CLEVER BY HALF;

OUTWITTED DEATH TILL HIS DYIN' BREATH
WHEN DEATH LAUGHED THE LAST LAUGH.

**SISYPHUS & MEN.**

YEAH, ROLL THE BOULDER UP THE HILL!
YEAH, PUT YOUR BACK INTO IT, Y'KNOW THE DRILL!
FORGET THAT SWEAT DRIPPIN' UNDER YOUR CROWN
'CAUSE WHEN YOU PUSH THAT BOULDER UP
THAT BOULDER ROLLS RIGHT DOWN.

**ALL WORKERS.**

O, MISERY AND WOE! AND WOE!
(BEAT, BEAT, BEAT, BEAT AND BROKEN SPIRITS.)
O, MISERY AND WOE! AND WOE!
(BEAT, BEAT, BEAT, BEAT AND BROKEN SPIRITS.)

**LITTLE LU.**

DANAUS HAD FIFTY DAUGHTERS:
EVIL – ALL BUT ONE,
SO FORTY-NINE DID "EIGHTY-SIX"
THEIR HUSBANDS JEST FOR FUN.

**DAUGHTERS OF DANAUS.**

DAUGHTER, FILL THE JUG WITH WATER.
POUR IT IN THE TUB NOW.
SQUEAKIN', GIRLS THIS TUB IS LEAKIN',
YOU'RE NEVER GONNA FILL IT,
NEVER GONNA FILL A TUB WITH NO BOTTOM,
NEVER GONNA WASH YOUR SINS WHEN YOU GOT 'EM,
POUR, BABY, POUR!

**ALL WORKERS.**

O, MISERY AND WOE! AND WOE!
(BEAT, BEAT, BEAT, BEAT AND BROKEN SPIRITS.)
O, MISERY AND WOE! AND WOE!
(BEAT, BEAT, BEAT, BEAT AND BROKEN SPIRITS.)

**LITTLE LU.**

BRUTUS BETRAYED HIS BEST PAL, CAESAR;
A "BACKSTABBER," Y'MIGHT SAY.
BUT A TRAITOR'S FALL IS THE WORST OF ALL
AND SO: *ET TU, BRUTE.*

**MEN.**

    IN THE MOUTH OF SATAN
    IS YOUR FATE AWAITIN',
    SATAN'S MASTICATIN'
    ON YOUR FLESH, MEN.
    FIRST WE'LL REND YOU
    THEN WE'LL MEND YOU
    THEN WE'LL SEND YOU
    BACK AGAIN!

**BRUTUS.** Ahhh!

    *(On a metal catwalk rising above the center of the warehouse.)*

    *(The* **ENSEMBLE [WOMEN]** *underscore with "O, MISERY AND WOE…!" as* **LITTLE LU** *speaks.)*

**LITTLE LU.** *(Handing her a putrid smock.)* All right let's git you over to this here conveyor belt. Yer gonna help Mr. Lethe cap his good. 'N' if this conveyor belt gets stopped up, I'm going to double-did you with my double-diddin' knife. And double-did means POOF, right out of *(French inflection.)* ex-is-TAHNS.

**AGNES.** What are you?

**LITTLE LU.** I'm Little Lu, and if you can believe it – I was an ANGEL ONCE! That's right pretty kitty, AN ANGEL!

    ANYONE CAN LOSE THEIR LIGHT;
    TAKE ME I FELL FROM GRACE!
    AND JUST LIKE YOU, I WOUND UP HERE –
    THIS CIRCLE'S A *HELL* OF A PLACE.

Now get to work! HyaH!

    *(The* **FACTORY WORKERS** *dance their enslavement as* **AGNES** *watches.)*

**AGNES.**

    NOW IT'S REAL.
    GET IN THE BED YOU MADE FOR YOURSELF.
    FATE WITH A SEAL,
    HERE IS THE PRICE AND YOU'VE PAID WITH YOURSELF.

OVER.
ALL MY HOPES ARE OVER,

| AGNES. | BRUTUS & LITTLE LU. | SISYPHUS. | DAUGHTERS OF DANAUS. |
|---|---|---|---|
| NOW IT'S | IN THE MOUTH OF SATAN | YEAH, ROLL THE | DAUGHTER, FILL THE JUG |
| REAL | | BOULDER UP THE HILL! | DAUGHTER, FILL THE JUG WITH WATER. |
| | IS YOUR FATE AWAITIN', | YEAH, PUT YOUR BACK | POUR IT IN THE TUB |
| GET IN THE BED | SATAN'S MASTICATIN' | INTO IT, Y'KNOW THE | NOW |
| YOU MADE FOR | | DRILL! | SQUEAKIN' GIRLS THIS |
| YOURSELF. | ON YOUR FLESH, MEN. | | TUB IS LEAKIN', |
| | | FORGET THAT SWEAT | YOU'RE NEVER GONNA |
| FATE WITH A | FIRST WE'LL REND YOU | DRIPPIN' UNDER YOUR | FILL IT, |
| SEAL, | | CROWN | NEVER GONNA FILL A TUB WITH |
| | THEN WE'LL MEND YOU | | NO BOTTOM |

HERE IS
THE

PRICE AND

YOU'VE
PAID
WITH
YOURSELF

JASPER!

THEN WE'LL
SEND YOU

BACK AGAIN

'CAUSE
WHEN
YOU
PUSH
THAT
BOULDER
UP
THAT
BOULDER
ROLLS
RIGHT
DOWN.

NEVER
GONNA
WASH
YOUR SINS
WHEN
YOU
GOT 'EM,

POUR BABY,
POUR!

**FACTORY WORKERS.**

O, MISERY AND WOE! AND WOE!
(BEAT, BEAT, BEAT, BEAT AND BROKEN SPIRITS.)
O, MISERY AND WOE! AND WOE!
(BEAT, BEAT, BEAT, BEAT AND BROKEN SPIRITS.)

**FACTORY WORKERS.**                    **LITTLE LU.**

O, MISERY AND WOE! AND                SHIFT!
  WOE!
(BEAT, BEAT, BEAT, BEAT AND
  BROKEN SPIRITS.)

**FACTORY WORKERS.**

O, MISERY AND WOE! AND WOE!
(BEAT, BEAT, BEAT, BEAT AND BROKEN SPIRITS.)

**MEN.**

WOE!

**LITTLE LU.** Git to work!

### [MUSIC NO. 24 "FACTORY SEQUENCE – PART 1"]

*(The daughters are working next to **AGNES**.)*

**A DAUGHTER** . When that psychotic redneck's not looking, drink the water. It'll take the edge off…

**AGNES.** What edge?

**A DAUGHTER.** It'll make you forget. You won't remember… anything. That's what the river water does… Makes you forget.

**AGNES.** I'll forget everything…and everyone?

**A DAUGHTER.** Quick, he's not looking. Drink!

**AGNES.**

> …SMALL DETAILS BEGIN TO BLUR,
> TILL THE PERSON THAT YOU WERE
> SEEMS SO DISTANT.
> WAS THAT YOU?
> AS EACH MEMORY ERASES,
> THE PHOTOS OF FAMILIAR FACES
> SMUDGE AND BLOT –
> BUT YOU WON'T CARE A LOT –!
> YOU'LL FORGET YOU FORGOT –!

> *(**LOKI** enters the factory floor and passes **LITTLE LU**. **AGNES** is distracted by their conversation.)*

**LITTLE LU.** Little Lu to Loki, come in

> *(As **LOKI**.)*

I am Loki.

Is Mr. Lethe done with that boy yet?

> *(As **LOKI**.)*

They're making the deal. Be done soon.

Ya! 'Cause I got an itchin' to double dead someone…

> *(Catches **AGNES** looking at them.)*

What're you lookin' at priddy kitty?! You best not stop up that machine or I'll make you a little less priddy!

> *(**AGNES** keeps to herself. She's getting an idea, building courage.)*

**AGNES.** Jasper. I've gotta save him.

> FALL IN, FALL IN.
> WHO'S TO SAY YOU'LL SURVIVE.
> FIND OUT HOW DEEP.
> LEARN THE SECRETS THEY KEEP
> AT THE BOTTOM WHERE YOU ARRIVE…

*(To the WORKER beside her.)*

**AGNES.** Stop capping the bottles.

**FACTORY WORKERS.** What?

**AGNES.** The belt will jam and we can escape!

**A DAUGHTER.** But after three thousand years, how can I stop? They'll…they'll…

**AGNES.** They'll what? The Norse Gods are on a break, it's just the redneck. Come on…*live a little.*

*(They stop capping. Ka-Put, Ka-Pow, Boom! The machine jams as AGNES steps back toward the daughters.)*

**LITTLE LU.** …The Hell is going on–?! You flooded the place. I got you now priddy kitty!

*(AGNES trips one of the DANAIDES, creating a domino of girls and water. Splash! Splash! The place floods!)*

*(SISYPHUS hesitates, then lets go of his giant boulder. It rolls downward, toward LITTLE LU and the machine.)*

*(LITTLE LU is crushed under the boulder. The factory is a disaster!)*

**A DAUGHTER.** Go, save your friend!

**A DAUGHTER.** Hey Hillbilly!

**LITTLE LU.** What?

**AGNES.** Which way to Mr. Lethe?

**FACTORY WORKERS.** That way!

**AGNES.** Thank you!

**A DAUGHTER.** Who's a priddy kitty now?

**A DAUGHTER.** Best. Day. Ever!

*(Mr. Lethe's office.)*

***[MUSIC NO. 25 "FACTORY SEQUENCE – PART 2"]***

*(Mr. Lethe's office, where **MR. LETHE** is habitually cutting paper with shredding scissors, as **MR. LETHE**'s secretary admits the goddess **HEL**, **JASPER** slung placidly over her shoulder like a pup.)*

**HEL.** Delivery, of the live boy!

**MR. LETHE.** *Thanks* Hel, you can just leave it there.

*(Then.)*

Please take a seat. Get in okay? I hope Loki and Hel weren't too rough with you. You can take the Norse Gods out of Valhalla but you can't take Valhalla out of the Norse Gods!

*(Laughs.)*

**JASPER.** What's, um. Going on?

**MR. LETHE.** Mr. Lethe… CEO of Lethe enterprises. Maker of that water you're so fond of. Gets rid of the headaches, don't it?

*(**JASPER** nods.)*

**JASPER.** I'm Daryl.

**MR. LETHE.** Daryl, no. Your name is Jasper.

**JASPER.** Jasper…

**MR. LETHE.** You're a "restart." Your memories have been erased. Let's see if we can fill that brain up again, boy.

*(Takes out file.)*

"Jasper was born to loving parents – though they were hardly loving to each other. He sometimes locked himself in his room as his parents were at each other's throats. Late at night, he could hear his mother talking softly into the phone to her 'boyfriend,' Todd…" Who fucks a Todd?

*(Then.)*

"And then there's Agnes: his one true love. Though he wouldn't believe it." Agnes: the girl he let drown. Oh, yes. It was all your fault, Jasper. Because you are incapable of loving anyone… And that's why she drowned…isn't it?

> *(Then.)*

**MR. LETHE.** Jasp-attack – can I call you that?

**JASPER.** No!

**MR. LETHE.** Jasp-attack, has anyone ever asked you the question?

### *[MUSIC NO. 26 "AWFUL PEOPLE"]*

WHAT IS LIFE?

**JASPER.** *(Voice-over.)* Life is awful people.

**MR. LETHE.** Yes…

WHAT *IS* LIFE?

THESE DAYS, THE KIDDIES,
THAT CESSPOOL OF YOUTH,
THEY SUCK THE TITTIES
FROM US, WHO'VE LONG KNOWN THE TRUTH.
THE BRATS FEED ON B.S.
WELL, AS LONG AS IT'S HOT.
THEY'RE *HATEFUL MONSTERS!* AND P.S.,
COMING FROM ME, THAT'S SAYING A LOT.

THEY ARE TOMORROW,
THEY'RE WHAT HEAVEN'S ALLOWED.
THEY RULE TOMORROW,
AND I COULDN'T BE MORE PROUD.

AWFUL PEOPLE, THEY AREN'T FLESH AND BONE.
NO: AWFUL PEOPLE, ARE CHEMIC'LLY GROWN.
YEP! AWFUL PEOPLE! AND EACH ONE A CLONE
AND THAT'S SWELL.
YEAH, YEAH, YEAH, YEAH,

AWFUL PEOPLE ARE PAVIN',
PAVIN' THE ROAD TO HELL.

I SEE THE CHITLIN'
OFF AND DID'LIN' OUTSIDE
THEY CHEW UP RIT'LIN,
FID'LIN', FIT TO BE TIED.

PARENTS USED 'EM AND SCREWED 'EM,
COUNTRY LEFT EACH ONE SCARRED,
BUT DO THEY OVERCOME IT? *NO – FACEBOOK!*
*"LIFE'S RULLY HARD..."*

**MR. LETHE.** Oh, life *is* a bitch, Jasper. But, think if you had some of my water up in the Living World. You could live in never ending bliss! Hell, I've been sending my other products up there for years.

**JASPER.** Other products?

**MR. LETHE.** Bourbon, Oxycontin, Heroin... You see, every time someone has a near-death experience, they take some of my products back with them. But now, I have someone who can transport themselves from the Living World to Deadland and back. I want *you* to be my rep up there! Get my water in the stores. Drink the water. Forget your life!

BRING ON TOMORROW!
THEY'RE THE BATTERS ON DECK.
GOTTA LOVE TOMORROW!
MAKES ME – *(Fake weeping.) JUST ONE SEC...*

AWFUL PEOPLE ASCEND TO THE THRONE,
BUT AWFUL PEOPLE, THEY CAN'T BE ALONE,
SO AWFUL PEOPLE SPAWN SOME OF THEIR OWN,
THEN, THEY DWELL.
YEAH, YEAH, YEAH, YEAH –
AWFUL PEOPLE ARE PAVIN', PAVIN' THE ROAD TO HELL
BUT...

**MR. LETHE.** ...If you help me, I'll let your little friend return to the Living World –

**JASPER.** And if I don't?

**MR. LETHE.** My current plan is to torture and torment her until she's pulp. But, of course she's used to that...

**JASPER.** What do you mean?

**MR. LETHE.** Oh, she's got deep dark secrets, my friend –

**JASPER.** Tell me!

**MR. LETHE.** No!

> AWFUL, AIN'T IT? BUT IT'S CARVED IN STONE
> THAT AWFUL CREATURES WILL RULE YOUR ZONE.
> THEY'RE AWF'LLY AWFUL, AS I THINK I'VE SHOWN…
> FOR YOU SEE – JASPER
>
> YOUR AWFUL PARENTS?!
> EACH AWFUL FRIEND?!
>
> YOUR AWFUL AGNES?!
> IT ALL CAN END, IF YOU AGREE,
> TO HELP THOSE AWFUL PEOPLE
> WITH THE MOST AWFUL SON-OF-A-BITCH:
> THAT'S ME!

> *(Then.)*

Do we have a deal?

> *(**LETHE**'s office.)*

> *(We hear **LOKI** over the intercom.)*

**LOKI.** *(Voice-over.)* Loki to Herr Lethe. Loki to Herr Lethe. Dere vas a tidal wave. De factories flooded. The vorkers are rioting!

**MR. LETHE.** AHHH! Time is of the essence, Jasper. Now sign!

> *(**AGNES** enters.)*

**AGNES.** Let him go!

### [MUSIC NO. 27 "FACTORY SEQUENCE – PART 3"]

**MR. LETHE.** Well, if it isn't the "Norma Rae" of the Underworld…

**AGNES.** You heard what I said…

**MR. LETHE.** Aw, you sound so forceful. You see, I just can't do that. Mister Jasper here is about to sign a contract to be my partner. Isn't that right, Jasper?

**JASPER.** *(To **AGNES**.)* Just go away. Now!

> WEIGHTLESS.
> I'M WEIGHTLESS DOWN HERE.

**AGNES.** Wait! Jasper, I want you to know something –

**MR. LETHE.** We don't have time for this.

**AGNES.** I shouldn't have tried to prove something to you –

**MR. LETHE.** Ooh! Daddy's little girl is so brave.

**AGNES.** What happened at the cliff –

**MR. LETHE.** She's going to leave you, just like your mother.

**AGNES.** No, that's not true. Remember the cliff…remember me…remember us.

**MR. LETHE.** Remember she said I love you and you can't love anyone.

**AGNES.** Listen… I shouldn't have pressured you. I shouldn't have said what I said that night.

**LETHE.** No one cares! No one cares about your problems! She's dead because of you.

**AGNES.** No! It's not your fault. I don't blame you for my death!

**JASPER.**

AGNES…

**MR. LETHE.** *(Dry-heaving sounds.)* Pathetic. Now sign!

*(We see the image of* **BEATRIX** *upstage. A memory.)*

**AGNES.** JASPER! You have the power to get us to Elysium. You have my heart inside you. You're a Half-life! You have one wish left.

**JASPER.** I wish…to go to Elysium!

**MR. LETHE.** Oh shit…

*(***JASPER*** throws the pen down and grabs* **AGNES.** *The world revolves around them.)*

## Scene Four: Elysium

*(The following voice-overs should be performed by members of the Ensemble.)*

**VOICE-OVER 1.** Her soul has been marked to move onto Elysium.

**VOICE-OVER 2.** It's where souls go to rest for eternity.

**VOICE-OVER 3.** I should take him on to Elysium and you back to the city.

**VOICE-OVER 4.** I wish…to go to Elysium.

**VOICE-OVER 5.** You have the ability to transport yourself…

**VOICE-OVER 6.** A half life.

*(Darkness continues.)*

**AGNES.** Jasper?

**JASPER.** Agnes…

*(The world around them slowly comes into focus. There is something peaceful about the whole scene. The air around them seems to glow. An endless meadow, a paradise at evening.)*

**AGNES.** You remember me…

**JASPER.** Yes.

*(Then.)*

It's you.

**AGNES.** It's me.

**JASPER.** I had forgotten what you looked like.

**AGNES.** I'm here.

**JASPER.** We're finally here… Together.

**AGNES.** Elysium.

**JASPER.** We have to find Pluto.

**AGNES.** And then we go home…

*(Memories seem to flood back to her; she stops.)*

To everything… Our lives… Friends… My stepmom… My father…

*[MUSIC NO. 28 "ELYSIUM"]*

*(Beat;* **AGNES** *hears the sounds of memories flooding back to her.)*

JASPER. What's wrong…?

AGNES. …All these memories are coming back to me… My pictures are going back on the wall… It's just a lot, ya know… The last picture is going back up…it's of… it's…

JASPER. Are you okay?

*(Beat.)*

Agnes.

AGNES. There are things about me you don't know… Jasper… I tried to tell you.

JASPER. I want to know.

AGNES. I can't.

JASPER. Tell me.

*(We hear peaceful music.)*

AGNES. It's so peaceful. What if we stayed here?

JASPER. What?

AGNES. I mean, what's back up there? Nothing. We could have a life down here –

JASPER. But is this a life…?

AGNES.
I'VE GOT NOTHING LEFT BUT A SOUL AND A BAG,
I'M LIVING DEAD.
MY COIL'S SPRUNG, AND MY BUCKET'S KICKIN'.
THERE'S NOTHING TO DO WHEN YOUR TIME'S FINISHED
 TICKIN'…

HERE I'VE FELT MORE FREE THEN I EVER DID.
TELL ME WHY I SHOULD GO BACK?

*(Then.)*

To my father and my stepmom…and the person I'm supposed to be…
WHY SHOULD I GO BACK?

**AGNES.**

> FAM'LY'S SHOULD CONNECT,
> THEY SHOULD SHARE RESPECT,
> BUT IT ALL FALLS THROUGH THE CRACK.

> *(Then.)*

Aren't I supposed to love them?

> *(Then.)*

Fact is, I don't. I don't love them. Is that wrong of me?

**JASPER.**

> NO, IT'S NOT WRONG.
> AND YOU'RE NOT ALONE;
> AND IT'S NOT LIFE AS YOU PLANNED

> *(Then.)*

My Mom cheated on my father. I was so angry at them both.

> NOT LIFE AS YOU PLANNED
> AND THEY SAY PRETEND,
> TRUST THE PAIN WILL MEND,
> THAT YOU'LL GROW AND UNDERSTAND.

But I have grown, and I thought it was my fault, but you know what, it wasn't.

**AGNES.**

> I WAS SO ALONE

**JASPER.**

> AGNES

> *(Then.)*

Tell me, Agnes…

**AGNES.** My father… He used to be nice… When Mom got sick he was so angry… Started out doing little things… grabbing my arm…and – I had to start wearing a lot of make-up to cover the… I think he hated me because I looked like Mom… He couldn't save her…the greatest doctor in the world couldn't save her…

> *(Beat.)*

JASPER. Agnes, I am so sorry… I didn't know…

AGNES. It was better that way…

> *(She takes out two Lethe water bottles.)*

We drink these and we forget everything.

JASPER. But, we'll forget each other…

AGNES. Maybe it's better, being dead is painful but maybe being alive hurts much more.

> **(JASPER** *takes the water. Each of them holding their poison.)*

**AGNES.**

WE'LL HAVE

**JASPER & AGNES.**

NOTHING LEFT

**AGNES.**

BUT A SOUL AND A BAG.

**JASPER & AGNES.**

TOGETHER, LIVING DEAD.

**AGNES.**

OUR

**JASPER & AGNES.**

COIL'S SPRUNG, AND THE BUCKET: KICKIN'.
AT LAST I'LL HAVE YOU

**AGNES.**

WHEN MY

**JASPER & AGNES.**

TIME'S FINISHED TICKIN'.

> *(After the song,* **AGNES** *seems frozen.)*

JASPER. Agnes? Agnes?

> *(The world goes dark except for* **JASPER** *and a new figure walking in the distance. It's* **THE GODDESS** *from before. The* **ENSEMBLE** *[as the* **ELYSIUM DEAD***] underscores the following dialogue with humming.)*

THE GODDESS. Do you like the music?

JASPER. What – what's happened to her?!

THE GODDESS. She has paused, only a moment. I asked you, do you like the music?

JASPER. It's haunting.

> *(Then.)*

Who are you?

THE GODDESS. I am the voice of the river, trapped forever. I was punished by Lethe because I tried to stop him from erasing memories…because I wanted to hold on to the last picture of my beloved…

> *(She stops, hearing the voices of the* **ELYSIUM DEAD** *all around her. She pulls the hood off her head.)*

JASPER. Who was your beloved?

THE GODDESS. Like your Agnes, I too, was lost. Like her, the one who loved me was given a chance to bring me home from the Underworld. But he failed. All that remains of my dearly beloved Orpheus is his song… yet I live eternally in death. I come to you now, Jasper, because I wish to save you, as he could not be saved.

JASPER. Eurydice?

EURYDICE. There is a song Jasper. You must hear it.

> *(The music grows louder as the* **ELYSIUM DEAD** *continue underscoring.)*

JASPER. I can't.

EURYDICE. You refuse.

JASPER. I lost my family!

> *(Then.)*

EURYDICE. It was meant to be.

JASPER. What about Agnes? What her father did to her! My parents! All the awful people! I'm through with it. There's nothing left up there for us…

EURYDICE. That's not true…

> **[MUSIC NO. 29 "LIFESONG"]**

**EURYDICE.**
>YOU WILL BE BURNED
>BUT YOU WILL SEE THE SUN.
>YOU WILL BEAR BLISTERS,
>ON YOUR FEET AS YOU RUN.
>BEFORE YOU'RE DONE,
>
>LET THERE BE LIFE.
>OH, LET THERE BE LIFE
>AND A SONG FOR ME
>ASK TO FEEL THE TOUCH,
>AND SWEAR YOU WON'T RESIST.
>YOU WILL BE CHEATED
>BUT YOU WILL BE KISSED.
>LET NOTHING BE MISSED,
>PLEASE SAY YOU'LL EXIST.
>
>AND LET THERE BE LIFE,
>AND A SONG FOR ME.
>
>THERE WILL BE NO MORE CONFUSING YOURSELF,
>NO REFUSING YOURSELF,
>NO MORE DELAYS.
>THERE'S ONLY THE CALL TO RESPOND TO,
>TASK TO GET ON TO,
>THE WORK OF YOUR DAYS.
>
>SO LET IT BEGIN
>AND ONE DAY, LET IT END.
>LET IT FALL TO PIECES,
>AND WHAT'S MEANT TO WILL MEND.
>WITH LIFE TO LEND
>AND DAYS TO SPEND
>
>JASPER,
>WITH YOUR BEST FRIEND,
>AGNES.
>IT'S YOUR CHANCE FOR
>LIFE
>LET THERE BE LIFE.
>LET THERE BE LIFE.
>LET THERE BE LIFE.

> TAKE BACK YOUR LIFE
> AND YOU CAN MAKE A SONG.

*(He looks up. She is gone.)*

**AGNES.** Jasper. Jasper. Hello?!

**JASPER.** I can't do this.

*(Then.)*

Something inside me allowed me to come after you. We have a chance to go back, somehow, and make something of our life. Together. I'm gonna bring you home.

**[MUSIC NO. 30 "PERSEPHONE'S GOODBYE"]**

*(Suddenly, statuesque **PERSEPHONE** bursts on, with suitcase, followed by stunted, fractured **PLUTO**. **VIRGIL** the lawyer dodders on, carrying with some difficulty a briefcase, folders, and various papers.)*

**PERSEPHONE.**

> GOODBYE!
> GOODBYE! PLUTO, GOODBYE!
> EYES DRY! DON'T YOU GO FALLING APART.
> WINTER RUN, COME SPRINGTIME, WE'RE DONE.
> AND ISN'T THAT WONDERFUL?

**PLUTO.** Persephone, my Snowflake! Don't go!

**VIRGIL.** *(He's looking for something.)* Uh, good afternoon, Pluto, your Highness, I'm here to discuss the um terms of your annual divorce. Let's see… "After spending half the year with you in Deadland and in her absence bringing Winter to the Living World, we confirm that Queen Persephone has fulfilled her obligation to you"…

*(Hands **PLUTO** the pen. He reluctantly signs.)*

…"And she may now return to the Living World, restoring Spring once again."

**PERSEPHONE.** Goodbye, Pluts. These six months were almost bearable.

*(He embraces her, not letting go;* **VIRGIL** *starts off, passing* **JASPER**, *who gets his attention.)*

**JASPER.** Virgil!

**VIRGIL.** Hey, Jasper! You made it!

**PLUTO.** Well, look who it is…the boy who's been upsetting the order of all of Deadland!

**JASPER.** Your highness, we want to go home.

**PERSEPHONE.** Jasper, there is only one living heart between you… Only one of you can go home… I'm sorry.

**JASPER.** But, you're a God! You could change anything that you want to!

**PLUTO.** Why should I help you or your miserable species? All you do is hurt one another. Husband to wife. Father to daughter. An endless cycle… Only one of you can go back. You must make the choice.

*(Beat.)*

**AGNES.** C'mon, Jasper, it's over.

**JASPER.** No, It's not over. I give up my life for her.

**AGNES.** Jasper! No!

**JASPER.** We have one live heart between us. I want her to have it.

### [MUSIC NO. 31 "LIFESONG – REPRISE"]

ASK TO FEEL THE TOUCH,
AND SWEAR YOU WON'T RESIST.
YOU'LL BE CHEATED
BY SOMEONE ELSE
YOU'LL BE KISSED.
LET NOTHING BE MISSED,
PLEASE SAY YOU'LL EXIST.

AND LET THERE BE LIFE,
AND A SONG FOR ME.

**AGNES.** No Jasper, you can't do this!

**JASPER.** Agnes, go back and live…and I will be here. Your best friend waiting for you. I've been afraid… Now I understand…

**AGNES.**

GOODBYE, JASPER. GOODBYE.

**JASPER.**

EYES DRY…

*(To* **PLUTO**.*)*

I'm ready.

**(PLUTO** *nods and goes to reach for his heart.)*

**PERSEPHONE.** Wait! *(Then.)*

Perhaps… *Darling*…a trade could be made for them.

**PLUTO.** What kind of trade?

### *[MUSIC NO. 32 "PLUTO"]*

**PERSEPHONE.** Jasper, Agnes. You long for Life, and not just any old life, but a "meaningful one." Consider my heart softened… As I make a sacrifice for you.

*(To* **PLUTO**.*)*

I'll stay. One more day of cold, *bitter* winter so they both can leave. For they now share one heart.

**PLUTO.** *(High-pitched squeal.)* Gasp!

Oh. Oh. Snowflake?! Really? Truly? Really?

**PERSEPHONE.** YES! I'll stay one more day so they can go.

**PLUTO.** Ahhhh! What a magical day this will be! I have to start planning all the super fun activities!

**(JASPER** *and* **AGNES** *glow dimly, both alive and both dead.)*

**PERSEPHONE.** Super fun activities…this is hell.

**AGNES.** Jasper!

**VIRGIL.** Always knew you had it in you, kid.

*(He exits.)*

**AGNES.** *(To* **PERSEPHONE**.*)* I don't know how I could possibly thank you enough.

**PERSEPHONE**. Well, it's not over yet, I'm afraid.

**PLUTO**. Oh right, you must make the dive and swim back through the River Lethe.

**PERSEPHONE**. And there you will face the ultimate test. For Jasper, you must lead Agnes through the river, but you must not look back at her, no matter what happens. If you do, you will lose her just like Orpheus lost Eurydice. You would never see each other again. So, think hard on this… Once you start, there is no return…

**PLUTO**.

WELL, GOOD LUCK, THANKS FOR COMING!

LET'S GO, MY QUEEN 'SEPHONE!

WON'TCHA HOLD MY HAND, AND SING, AND SKIP HOME
WITH ME?

**PERSEPHONE**.

THANK GODS IT'S JUST ONE DAY…

**PLUTO**.

TRA LA LA LA LA LA LAAAAA

> (**PLUTO** *and* **PERSEPHONE** *skip off.* **AGNES** *and* **JASPER** *look out; beat.*)

**JASPER**. Are you ready for this…?

**AGNES**. You can never be certain about anything in life… but that's okay.

**JASPER**. Yeah… That's okay…

### [MUSIC NO. 33 "THE SWIM"]

AND WE WON'T DARE LOOK BACK

**JASPER & AGNES**.

AND WE WON'T DARE LOOK BACK

**JASPER & RIVER LETHE**.

JUST MEET ME AT THE TOUCH OF WATER

FOR ONE MORE LAP WITH ME.HA-AH, HA-AH HOO

**AGNES**.

WE'LL PULL THROUGH THE BLACK,

**JASPER**.                 **SOLO SOPRANO**.

AND WE WON'T LOOK BACK      AH

**AGNES.**        **SOLO TENOR.**
 WE'LL KEEP OUR STYLE   AH
 THROUGH THE MILLIONTH
  MILE,

**JASPER & AGNES.**
 AND WHEN IT'S MORE THAN
 WE CAN STAND –

  (**JASPER** *and* **AGNES** *disappear into The River.*
  **MR. LETHE** *appears. He pulls* **AGNES.** **JASPER**
  *hears the* **VOICES OF DOUBT** *cascade all around*
  *him.*)

**JASPER & AGNES.**
 WE'LL GO STROKE BY STROKE

        **MEMORIES.**
 BY STROKE BY STROKE BY  AH
  STROKE

        AH

**JASPER.**   **AGNES.**   **RIVER LETHE.**
 WEIGHTLESS  WE'LL GO   STROKE
 WERE    STROKE
 WIGHTLESS  BY STROKE BY  BY STROKE
 AGNES!   STROKE   BY STROKE
 BY STROKE BY BY STROKE BY BY STROKE
 STROKE   STROKE   BY STROKE

           **SOLO BOY**
**JASPER.**   **AGNES.**   **RIVER LETHE.** **& SOLO GIRL.**
 YOU'RE   NEVER ALONE!  STROKE   AH
 NEVER
 ALONE!
 YOU'RE   NEVER ALONE!  BY STROKE
 NEVER         BY STROKE
 ALONE!

          BY STROKE
          BY STROKE
 YOU'RE   NEVER ALONE!
 NEVER
 ALONE!

**JASPER.**

> AGNES?! AGNES?!
> I'LL SAVE YOU AGNES…

**EURYDICE.**

> HELLO, JASPER… HELLO

> *(**AGNES** has disappeared – we only see **JASPER**.)*

**EURYDICE.** Don't look back Jasper, she's there, she's always been there. Remember the song.

**JASPER.**

> OH LET IT BEGIN
> AND ONE DAY, LET IT END.
> LET IT FALL TO PIECES,
> AND WHAT'S MEANT TO WILL MEND.
> WITH LIFE TO LEND
> AND DAYS TO SPEND FOR LIFE.

## Scene Five: Back Up Here

*(The base of the cliff, on shore.* **JASPER** *is pulling* **AGNES** *out of the water. She isn't moving.)*

**JASPER.** Agnes! Please don't die. Please. I am sorry. I should have been there…

*(Then.)*

I'D GIVE MY LIFE…
I'D GIVE MY LIFE…
I'D GIVE MY LIFE –
TO SHARE WITH YOU A SONG…

I love you.

*(We see* **PERSEPHONE.** *She hears* **JASPER** *say this, and she is taken in by what she has seen and his courage. She begins to make it snow.* **AGNES** *awakens, gasping for breath.)*

Agnes!

**AGNES.** Jasper? I… I did it. I jumped in. You would have been so proud of me…

**JASPER.** I am, I am proud of you…

**AGNES.** But, when I hit the water, I tried to get back to shore, but I couldn't… I just…it was so hard. Harder than I thought it would be… But, you weren't here, Jasper –

**JASPER.** I'm here now. For you. For good.

*(He kisses her.)*

**AGNES.** That was…unsolicited. And why is it snowing? And in the middle of spring?

**JASPER.** An act of God, I guess. Or Goddess.

### [MUSIC NO. 34 "ONE MORE DAY OF SNOW"]

**JASPER.**

MY TOES ARE BOUND TO BREAK OFF.
MY NOSE WILL CRACK IF I COUGH.
BUT OH, LOOK AT THE SNOW…

*(The snow falls harder as other warmly-dressed* **TEENAGERS** *walk the streets, holding their iPads and iPhones. Suddenly, they all look up at the snow and start to slowly put their electronics away. They start dancing in the snow, falling into snowdrifts, doing snow angels.)*

EACH DRIFT IS SHOVELED AND CURBED
EACH LIFE COMPLETELY DISTURBED
AND ALL THE WORLD TAKES STOCK
AS ICE EVEN FREEZES THE CLOCK –

THE YEARS ARE GETTING SHORTER,
BUT I AM GROWING TALL.
LET THESE CLOUDS PART SLOWLY –
WE'VE GOT NOWHERE TO GO;
THERE'S ONE MORE DAY OF SNOW.

**TEEN SOLO #1.**

THE POWER GOES IN THE GALE:

**TEEN SOLO #2.**

NO NET, NO TV, NO MAIL.

**TEEN SOLO #3.**

WE'RE LOST UNDER THE FROST.

**TEEN SOLO #4 & #5.**

SO OUT THE DOOR TO THE STREET

**TEEN SOLO #6.**

TO FIND A FRIEND IN THE SLEET.

**ALL.**

AND THROUGH THE FLURRY OF FLUFF,

**TEEN SOLO #7.**

I THINK WE DON'T SLOW DOWN ENOUGH…

| **AGNES.** | **JASPER & TEENAGERS.** |
|---|---|
| IT SEEMS AS LIFE GROWS SHORTER, | OOH |
| IT GETS HARDER WALKING TALL. | OOH |

**AGNES, JASPER & TEENAGERS.**

BUT DAYS WHEN
FLAKES ARE FLOWING –

**AGNES.**

>  ARE THE BEST I KNOW,
>  HERE'S TO DAYS AND DAYS OF
>  SNOW.

**JASPER & TEENAGERS.**

>  DAYS AND DAYS

**JASPER & TEENAGERS GROUP 1.**

>  THESE YEARS ARE GETTING SHORTER

**AGNES & TEENAGERS GROUP 2.**

>  THESE YEARS ARE GETTING SHORTER,

**JASPER & TEENAGERS GROUP 1.**

>  AND I AM GROWING TALL,

**AGNES & TEENAGERS GROUP 2.**

>  AND I AM GROWING TALL,

**JASPER & TEENAGERS GROUP 1.**

>  LET THESE CLOUDS PART SLOWLY –

**AGNES & TEENAGERS GROUP 2.**

>  CLOUDS PART SLOWLY –

**AGNES, JASPER & TEENAGERS.**

>  GRAB A FIST TO THROW,
>  THERE'S ONE MORE DAY OF SNOW!

>  (**JASPER** *and* **AGNES** *dance together as the* **TEENAGERS** *play in the snow.*)

**TEENAGERS.**

>  LA LA LA LA LA LA
>  LA LA LA LA LA LA LA LA LA
>  LA LA LA
>  LA LA LA LA LA LA
>  LA LA LA LA LA LA LA LA
>  LA LA LA

>  (**TEENAGERS** *continue underscoring with "La La."*)

**ASPER & AGNES.**

>  FOR THE LOVE OF MY LIFE
>  THIS IS THE LOVE OF MY LIFE
>  I LOVE MY LIFE!
>  FOR THE LOVE OF MY LIFE
>  YOU ARE THE LOVE OF MY LIFE

I LOVE MY LIFE!

> *(**AGNES** and **JASPER** fall into the snow together, and he lays his head in her lap.)*

**JASPER.**                              **TEENAGERS.**

    THE DAY IS GETTING SHORTER.    OOH

    THERE'S NOT MUCH TIME AT ALL.    OOH

**JASPER.**

    I'LL LOVE MY FATE, AND I'LL

**JASPER & AGNES.**

    LOVE MY LIFE,

    EVER AS WE GO,

**OTHERS.**

    EVER AS WE GROW,

    AND THE ONLY TRUTH WE KNOW:

**OTHERS.**

    ONLY TRUTH WE KNOW:

    TODAY'S A DAY…

    …FOR SNOW.

> *(The children play. Fade to black.)*

> *(Curtain.)*

www.ingramcontent.com/pod-product-compliance
Lightning Source LLC
Chambersburg PA
CBHW071929130726
47909CB00014B/2700